CAUTIONARY TALES

EMMANUELLE DE MAUPASSANT

Edited by
ADREA KORE

First published in 2016

www.emmanuelledemaupassant.com

DEDICATION

This collection of tales bawdy, haunting, horrific and erotic is dedicated to the lovely Ms. Kore. Each story bloomed under her caress. Although these tales have been long in the writing, they appear in their current form only because of the life breathed into them by my editor extraordinaire, my friend, Adrea.

Her expertise drew out these tales of deceit, vanity, greed and lust. Her eye saw to the heart of the themes, and how best to convey them to you, my reader. She heard the voices of our narrative ghosts, bringing them so vividly to the page. This collection is not only mine but hers.

This work is also dedicated to tellers of tales through the ages, to all who have entertained and shared their wisdom. It is dedicated to Homer, to Chaucer and to Boccaccio, to Angela Carter and to Fay Weldon, all of whom have inspired elements of these stories.

These tales draw upon the customs and superstitions of the Slavonic lands of Eastern Europe. They are not retellings, being brewed from my imagination, but are seasoned with motifs and mythologies which will be familiar to any who have lived or travelled in this part of the world.

ABOUT CAUTIONARY TALES

The boundaries between the everyday and the unearthly are snakeskin-thin. The trees have eyes and the night has talons. Demons, drawn by the perfume of human vice and wickedness, lurk with intents malicious and capricious. Tread carefully, for the dark things best left behind in the forest may seep under your door and sup with you. The lover at your window or in your bed may have the scent of your death already on their breath.
Is the shadow on the wall, really yours, after all?

'Funny, brutal, and irreverent' – Bustle.com

Twelve tales inspired by Eastern European and Russian superstitions and folklore; darkly delicious imaginings for the adult connoisseur of bedtime stories.

FOREWORD

We are the voices in the shadows,
    Between the light and shade,
    Betwixt life and restful death,
    In the dark periphery of the unseen.

We're here,
    At the edges.
    We are the villainous punished,
    The innocent murdered or abandoned,
    Our lives ended by foul means, or unspeakable deeds.
    We are your lovers long gone; your siblings forsaken.

Can you hear us?
    At the edges

In life - jealous, greedy, vain,
    Hearts black-secreted,
    Our fingers, ever-clutching,

At what was never ours.

In death – we do not lie easy in quiet graves.
    We watch from beyond and behind and below,
    In the realm of the malevolent, the vengeful,
    Unwillingly abed with lurking forces of malice.

Here, at the edges,
    Whispering to you,
    And we're not alone; not alone
    Here, in the dark.

We are behind the door, in the corners,
    In the room where you've just extinguished the light.
    We flicker in the shadow you cast on the wall.
    We are the prickle on the back of your neck.
    Curled, in words unspoken,
    We are the shiver on your uneasy flesh,
    The creep of the unknown on your skin.

Can you feel us?
    Here, at the edges.

Seek us in the flames of the fire in your hearth.
    Seek us in the dark breath of the forest,
    In the waters at the bottom of your well,
    In the fog, and the streams and the marshes.
    We are watching,
    From the edges.

All of nature now our cousins,
 We may pass through and dwell within
 The squeak of the mouse,
 And the crow's beady eye,
 The crawling of lice,
 And the buzz of the fly.

Wrapped in our anger, and desire for revenge,
 We do not rest.
 We are the rebellious dead,
 Damned and damning,
 Seeped in blood and steeped in poison,
 Devoured and skinned,
 Filled with hate.

Peace will never be ours,
 We suffered foul means and violent demise.
 Now, who will pay?
 Who will pay?

We tell these stories because we must,
 We tell these stories, for now we know.
 The old ways have wisdom;
 the old customs served to keep us safe.
 Take heed: Remember the old ways.

Here, from the edges, we see all life,
 from birth to death.
 We see daily labours and bread,
 all between hearth and bed,

We see love, and lust, and loathing,
We know now what feeds upon it,
Oh, too well we know.

Hear our stories, learn from our errors.
We too were once flesh, and blood:
Ignoble impulses.
'Tis a folly all too human,
to presume you know better.
Take heed: remember the old ways.

We were of this world, but no more,
We are beyond this world, evermore.
Beyond life, yet not quite in death,
Watching, watching,
from the edges.

As those who have come before and will ever be,
We know the secrets of nature,
and of human hearts.
We know what lies beneath,
in the hidden corners of your soul,
and we know who watches alongside us.

We did not escape them in life,
and they shadow us still beyond death.
We are watching; they are watching,
here, at the edges.

Ambition, envy and greed: we know what you covet,

and what you covet
draws them ever nearer,
Bringing endless despair, and your own demise.

Crook your finger;
    they'll come closer.
    Pull the covers tighter to your chin;
    in beside you they'll creep.

Listen,
    listen with your eyes,
    and your lips.
    Listen with your skin,
    and your blood.
    Can you hear us,
    at the edges?

You who lust after wealth,
    You who crave illicit pleasures of the flesh,
    You who spin deceit,
    Beware.

Good and evil exist in all of us.
    a moment's temptation takes us on a wrong path.
    On that path may lurk foul fiends,
    inhuman, yet feeding, needing
    all our weaknesses: vanity, indolence and envy,
    Easy fruits for evil appetites,
    our flesh, a tasty afterthought,
    our bones flung asunder.

Here, at the edges, we see what you cannot.
 We are not alone, and nor are you.
 Hear our stories: take heed.
 We watch, but the demons watch too.

They were watching us.

AGAINST MURDER

The Likho is an evil one-eyed fiend from the forest, known for its fondness for human flesh.

A moment's temptation
takes us on a wrong path.
On that path may lurk foul fiends.

A DAIRY FARMER was once married to a woman so cantankerous and contrary that there was no living with her. If he asked her to get up early and help him milk the cows, she'd lie in bed until noon. If he requested pancakes, she'd be sure to cook beetroot soup. If he dared suggest that she muck out the cowshed, he'd find a pile of dung in his boots.

She found constant fault: his breath reeked of garlic and his armpits of onions; his back was an eruption of boils; he always had grease in his beard and cabbage between his teeth; and he slurped food like an animal. One night, she went too far, scoffing that he was useless between the sheets, since no children had ever been conceived there.

'I'd rather share my bed with a pig!' she complained.

Driven beyond all patience, he took a pillow and held it over her head until her arms flailed no more. It took but a minute and, immediately, a blissful hush settled on the house. He wondered why he'd never thought of it before.

Of course, when evil thoughts and deeds are abroad, they attract certain creatures and crawlers, as we restless spirits know all too well. Man's wicked folly draws them close.

A malevolent forest demon, the *Likho*, sniffed the scent of violence and came creeping from its winter lair, bare feet stepping steadily through the snow. Dark lips contorted in a grin of anticipation, revealing yellow teeth and blackened tongue.

The fiend headed into the village and, as was its wont, paused to check upon the hens. It stroked those sitting on an uneven number of eggs, its filthy talons tickling where it might have rent asunder. Claws trailing over fences and gates, it made its inevitable path, drawn towards the stench of ill deeds.

Finally, the beast arrived at the house of the dairyman. It peeked through the shutters with its one eye and there, by the morning light, watched as the husband laid out his wife on the table, so that her feet faced the door, as was the custom.

The dairyman tucked her nightgown round her toes and opened the window a little, despite the nip of frosty air.

'Off you go,' he declared, 'Fly away elsewhere.'

On the beams above the warm stove, the ghost of the murdered woman sat grumpily, glaring down at her husband, quite as she had done in life.

So it is that we, the unhappily departed, are often obliged to haunt the places of our damnable demise. Little does man know of this shadowed realm, between light and dark, and the torments that bind us so closely to the world where once we drew breath.

Having dispatched his wife, the dairyman's thoughts turned to the shapely widow next door. With a spring in his step, he donned his best shirt and hat, and sauntered round to see her, intending that they be married as soon as the burial rites were completed.

The widow was flattered by the alacrity of his proposal, considering that breath had barely left the wife's body, and accepted gladly. So eager was the hussy to take the woman's place that she suggested moving in straight away – on the pretext of cleaning and cooking for him in his time of distress.

The *Likho* had waited until the man walked down the path and had slithered in through the open window, surveying the fresh corpse and the ghost, still hunched above and scowling.

'Ha!' cackled the fiend, 'I expect you'd like revenge on that husband of yours. Murder shouldn't go unpunished, and no creature enjoys delivering chastisement as much as I. What about giving him a taste of his own medicine? If you'd be so kind as to lend me your body, I'll set him dancing to my tune.'

The wife's spectre grimaced and nodded, at which the wicked *Likho* stripped off the nightgown, then the dead woman's pliant skin, peeling back the flaccid folds. These it left in a slack heap.

It gobbled her flesh and sucked the bones clean. These it hid behind the stove, before inserting itself inside the empty, wrinkled carcass, taking the former position of the corpse. Its fat tongue swiped the last juices from around its lips.

When the husband returned home, all was as it had been; there was not a speck of blood to be seen, although the strangest smell of rotten eggs lingered.

The neighbours came to pay their respects and offer condolences, and the comely widow served pancakes and *pirozhki* dumplings to the mourners. A few eyes rolled; it required no fortune telling to see which way the wind was blowing. However, life goes on, and the villagers agreed that the new couple were a good match. His first wife had been a harridan, with few good words for anyone; none would miss her.

Once the guests had left, it wasn't long before the man and the floozy tumbled into bed, tittering and fondling. So intent were they that neither noticed the corpse sitting up to watch them.

After some minutes, the *Likho* called out, 'That hardly seems polite. I've only been dead a few hours.'

The widow screamed and the dairyman jumped up so quickly that his head cracked on the ceiling. Both assumed that the corpse had returned to life to berate them.

Kneeling on the floor, the man pleaded with his departed wife for forgiveness. At this, the widow raised an eyebrow. She'd been ignorant of bedding a murderer, although the news was no real surprise.

The *Likho* raised the corpse's mouth in a leer, replying, 'Not to worry. I'll join you. I'm sure there's room for three. My feet are cold, so I'd appreciate you warming them for me.'

With that, the devilish creature hopped into bed and patted the covers, indicating that the husband should clamber in. The fiend lay between the two, a cold hand placed on the thigh of each. It then went to sleep, snoring loudly through the night, while the pair lay awake, too horrified to move or speak. The strumpet could hardly deny that she'd climbed into her neighbour's bed more quickly than etiquette allowed, and now she was facing the consequences.

In the morning, the corpse sat at the table and declared to the widow, 'I'm feeling quite peckish. I suppose you can cook? A plate of draniki if you please and look sharp about it.'

Too terrified to argue, the woman began her task. Each draniki she set down was gobbled in a single gulp, replaced by the demand for more. The *Likho* rapped the husband's knuckles when he tried to take one, telling him to wait until it'd had its fill. Eventually, every potato in the house had been eaten.

'I'm still rather hungry,' admitted the corpse. 'Why don't you go and shoot some rabbits? We might have a stew.' It inclined its head towards the door, to indicate that the husband had better get a move on.

As soon as he had departed, the *Likho* sat back in the chair contentedly. 'I suggest that you milk the cows while he's gone and then clean the house,' the corpse commanded.

All day, the widow tended to the animals, scrubbed and polished, until she was ready to swoon. As soon as the *Likho* saw this, it clapped its hands in glee and split the woman neatly in two with a flick of its talons.

Such are the rewards of those who crave illicit pleasure and who care not how their comforts are attained. A moment's temptation takes us on a wrong path, on which may lurk foul fiends.

As before, it feasted on the tender flesh and licked the bones clean. The skin it put to one side and, casting off the wrinkled wrapper of the murdered wife, slipped inside the new.

The demon tossed the bedraggled old remnants behind the stove, with all the bones, and gave itself a shake, adjusting to its new costume. It preferred the shape of this skin, which was smoother and altogether more plump and comfortable.

It winked at the wife's ghost, still perched overhead.

'Don't worry. I've not forgotten him!' the fiend assured her.

When the man returned (without any rabbits, since all had eluded his gun and traps) he was delighted to see that the animated corpse of his old wife had departed and that his new ladylove appeared in good spirits.

'My darling, I persuaded her to leave,' cooed the demon. 'Now, come and give me a kiss.'

The *Likho* locked him in a firm embrace and wrestled him onto the bed.

'Goodness me,' exclaimed the dairyman. 'Gentle my

love. You're like a bear tonight. You'll crush the breath out of me.'

The beast gave a girlish giggle. 'If I'm a bear then you must be my honey,' it simpered.

It squeezed the man so tightly that he fell into a faint. In a trice, he was rent down the middle, becoming a tasty supper for the evil creature. Once the flesh had been gobbled, the *Likho* stuffed the skin and bones behind the stove and retired to bed.

At dawn, the demon sprang awake, ready to see what the day might bring. By the door, it noticed a basket of mushrooms, brought from the forest by the dairyman the day before. With a flip of the pan, the fiend fried up the delicacies, serving them with a dollop of sour cream and swallowing them utterly in three great gulps.

So self-satisfied was the beast that it hadn't noticed the basket brimming only with poisonous varieties: chosen by the dairyman in hope of finally sending his corpse wife into the hereafter.

The creature clutched its stomach, torn by a churning ache. Such was its torment that the *Likho* flung off the widow's skin and bolted out of the door, back to the forest.

It left behind an empty house, but for the graveyard behind the stove and the shrivelled casing of the floozy, cast onto the floor.

As for the wife's disgruntled spirit, it had found the past days' events more than agreeable and was content, at last, to leave.

. . .

GLOSSARY

Pirozhki: small baked or fried pies, filled with vegetables, meat or fruit

Draniki: potato cakes (grated then fried) – usually served with sour cream

AGAINST FAITHLESSNESS

THERE WAS ONCE a handsome and wealthy young man whose self-love surpassed that of any love he ever bestowed on another. Whether through folly, or pride, or vanity, he found none deserving of his true affection. He roamed the land, seeking out the prettiest of companions, much as he would hunt deer or boar in the woodlands.

Women allowed him all liberties, flattered by his gifts and honeyed words, and would offer their hearts readily. Yet, though he oft thought himself in love for some short while, he soon tired of their embraces. He would leave always in the dead of night, stepping over them as they slept, to avoid the unpleasantness of formal parting.

With spring comes the unfurling of verdant buds and the stretching of long-dormant beasts. At such times do huntsmen go in search of meat, just as evil forces sniff out the selfish, the deceitful, and the greedy for their prey.

As the young man passed, a rabbit appeared from under a bush. It looked at him with sage eyes beady.

'A tasty morsel for my belly,' thought he, and leapt down from his horse to seize its ears.

It hopped away, but only just out of reach. The eager hunter bounded forward but, once more, the rabbit escaped him.

Each time he went to grasp the dainty creature, it loped beyond his clutches, then waited, as if urging him to catch up.

In this way, he was lured into the forest, into the darker depths, further than he had ever been before, and the time passed more quickly than he realised. His horse he had left behind in his compulsion to follow the devious rabbit.

Whose eyes looked upon him from within that innocent creature?

Not ours.

At last, with dusk approaching, he found himself in a glade. The rabbit, having continued to elude him, now disappeared altogether. Noticing a light shining through the trees, he approached, and saw smoke emerging from the chimney of a cottage.

He could have turned back but, having come so far, he felt curious to discover who lived in the cottage. He drew nearer, until his chin was resting upon the very ledge of the window, its shutters folded open.

And we, from within the sigh of the trees, and the soft moss underfoot, and the calling of night birds, watched him as he watched, gazing where he should not.

Inside, there was a bed, and upon the bed there was a woman. More beautiful was she even than the damask rose while her scent, drifting through the open window, was that of the night dew. Her hair was silken as the raven's wing. Quite naked, she lay, so still upon the bed, her eyes closed in reverie.

The young man looked first upon her breasts, where her hand rested. And upon each breast, there was a rosebud nipple. Upon each nipple there was a tip most tender. Upon each tip there was a milky drop.

Chin lifted, lips parted, she milked her maiden breast.

'What I would give to suckle at that teat,' thought he. 'This lady, so pure and good, may be worthy of my love.'

She raised her knee and moved her hand to her belly, down, down, to cup between her legs.

'What I would give to kiss that sweet cunt,' thought he. 'This lady, so passionate, may be worthy of my love.'

He stayed at the window, watching the lady press her fingers within her velvet cave.

At that moment, she opened her eyes and, turning her head towards the window, looked at the lad directly, as if she had known all along he were there (which perhaps she had).

She did not flinch or frown. She smiled: a knowing smile, of one who sees far more than they show.

He felt some shame at being so discovered, but also inflamed, as the lady fair watched him now, with her eyes of deepest jade. As her fingers played upon her sex, she held his gaze, unblinking, even to the moment when the tight coil in her belly unravelled, and she uttered her cry, as if all were for him.

She covered herself then in furs, came out to take his hand, and led him inside.

'Don't speak,' said she. 'You wished to see me and so

you shall. I'll show you more than any man, if here you'll stay and be my love.'

She gazed into his eyes and saw they were full of longing. With that she dropped her furs and lay down with him before the fire, and showed him all she promised, wrapped close in kisses.

'Here at last is a lady worthy of my love,' thought he.

And from those flames of the hearth, we watched, as the lad suckled at her breast so pale and drank the milk of her fatal spell. We sent a prickle to the back of his neck, the creep of the unknown to his skin. But he no heed, so wholly was his attention upon his seductive lover. Languor fell upon him as the nectar dripped, and took him down into a dark realm.

The siren sheathed his ready manhood, taking him on a dance of rhythmic power. She milked him of his seed all through the witching hours, even as he fell to dreaming. There, in his slumber, he thought himself upon a bed of velvet, a bed of flesh. As he writhed, that soft and yielding place surrounded him, so that he sank ever deeper. And still that silky flesh caressed him, engulfing waves upon his naked body, a chamber of ecstasy and raw desire.

With the morning sun, he awoke and found his lady's limbs bare and cool. She lay quite still, sleeping so deeply that she could not be roused.

'My love!' he cried, thinking her dead. 'Do not forsake me! So long I've looked for one such as you!'

The lady shifted then in her slumber, and let forth a gentle sigh.

Such relief the young man felt, though still perturbed by the duration and depth of her strange sleep.

Believing that she would wake in good time, he covered her with a quilt, and set himself a breakfast of gingerbread, nuts and sweet berry jam.

Still she slept.

He wandered outside, first chopping firewood, then feeding the stove.

Still she slept.

He lay down beside her, to watch her sleeping breaths, and let his hand creep beneath the quilt. How smooth her skin, and how fragrant her hair, as if she were made of iris petals, rather than human substance. As his hand traced its path, he felt his manhood rising.

He placed his mouth upon her breast.

He placed his cock between her thighs.

He buried deep in that fleshy den, and rode her to his pleasure.

Having taken his fill, he fell at last to slumber.

As the corncrakes began their early evening melody, the lady stirred. He too awoke, with great happiness at finding her restored.

He began at once to ask why she had slept so long, and, being honest in some ways, though not in others, told her how he had attempted to rouse her in the best way he knew how.

'My eager one,' she chided. 'How sweet were your caresses while I slept, but all too short. I felt every touch upon my skin, and each sweet piercing. I beg, fear not to stint in your attentions, should you find me so again.'

She drew him to her, as if she would eat his very soul.

Here, at the edges, we see what you cannot.

> We see love, and lust,
> Easy fruits for evil appetites.
> We know what feeds upon them.

So liberally he washed her with his seed that he fell once more into sleep, and woke to find her in some other realm, beyond rousing. He ate a simple meal, then walked out to take the air, and to collect the earliest of berries.

No matter where he turned, he came upon the clearing within which the cottage sat, as if his feet were governed by some force not his own.

As before, he counted the hours, impatient for her awakening, until, recalling his lady's request to make love to her as she slumbered, he entered her bed.

Only the faintest rising of her chest evinced life yet within her.

He placed his mouth upon her belly.

He placed his mouth upon her cunt.

He placed his tongue inside her cave.

And he drank.

There dripped the sweetest ambrosia, and the more he lapped, the more there flowed, inspiring him to greater fervour. His mouth worked ardently, and without respite, until his jaw quite began to ache, and yet he could not stop. As if enchanted by the potion of her sex, he continued to sweep his moist caress within those fleshy gates. His tongue-tip played upon her nub and stroked, and soothed, drawing ripples of delight through her womb, and the softest of moans from those sleeping lips.

Here, at the edges, we see what you cannot.
Pull the covers tighter to your chin
We know who'll creep in beside you.
We aren't alone, and nor are you.

He knew not how much time had passed but, at last, the light began to fade and his lady woke, releasing him from the strange compulsion which had overtaken him.

Wearied, his eyes would close but his beloved would not let him rest.

'Think not to sleep until I've had my pleasure,' said she.

Her lips closed about his cock and, with each stroke of her mouth, his engorgement grew. He felt the stretch of skin and pulse of blood, and still she sucked, causing him to swell and swell, to a size quite double that he'd seen before. The sight filled him with both pride and fear.

'This shaft is mine to command,' she smiled. 'And now you'll oblige me in all I ask.'

She climbed upon his lap and took his sword, inch by inch, until it filled her well. The undulations of those hips had their own enchantment, unrelenting. Faster now, and deeper, harder, she rode him without care or caution. In her abandon, hair out-streaming, he caught a glimpse of something hidden: something darker, cold, cunning. She harboured a lust, perversely frenzied; his pleasure nought against her taking.

So passed the hours of wanton copulation, he being powerless to resist. His body endlessly obliged the lady's hunger until, once more, the young man fell into the oblivion of sleep, she riding still upon his swollen cock.

This time, his dream brought a vision of his lover rocking slow upon him, serpentine in her embrace, gripping his girth, her cunt a devouring python. Her mouth lowered, soft and welcoming, coaxing from him the sweetest kiss. Then, in dread, he saw those lips peel back. Fangs raked, to release his blood, and her tongue flicked at the ruby droplets. She suckled now from him.

HE WOKE to the lady sleeping, her face in such repose that he wondered whether his captive fornication of the night were but a dream. Nevertheless, the ache in his groin and the weariness in his bones did not lie. He snatched his clothes and made to leave that place, intent on freedom.

He took but three steps towards the door, then felt a mighty jerk within his groin, as if a string were being tugged most violently, pulling him back, and back, and back.

His hands began to itch, each fingertip a burning ember. Against his true desire, his body crept, back to his lover, back to the bed.

'What torment is this?' cried the man. 'Am I a prisoner? What is this curse?'

No answer was there, as his captor slept.

His fingers blazed all the same, drawn to that cavern of dark delights, that garden fierce, his cage, his grave. The lady sighed and parted her pale thighs, inviting his touch, his blistering flame. And there within, as his fingers met her smooth flesh, he found cool respite to ease his pain.

What use are words when power they lack? Sobs and entreaties were to no avail.

He was hers, under her spell.

The hours passed, his fingers at her bidding, caressing, kneading. Tears came, departed and dried, until the hour of her wakening arrived. Her face was stony as she looked upon him. She taunted, 'Am I no longer your true beloved?'

He could only look away, no more wishing to see her face, but she had not finished with her prey, and grasped his chin, to force his gaze.

The soft skin he had caressed hung now in folds, her lips scabrous and eyes clouded, her voice, once tender, now scratched with despise. Here was her true self: witch-seductress hag, and hunter of men.

> Here at the edges, we see what you cannot.
> We see love and lust and loathing.
> We know what feeds upon them

'You will look upon me for as long as I choose it to be so. Look upon me and remember those women you have loved and left behind. Such faithlessness deserves remembrance by one who promises always to be faithful to you.'

She bent close, that he might inhale the rank breath of her yellow-toothed grin. Her sagging breast, so wrinkled, she lifted to his face, and the coarse, encrusted nipple to his waiting lips. She squeezed that foul udder as she had the first night of their meeting, that he might drink the sour milk within.

> Here at the edges, we see what you cannot.
> We are not alone, and nor are you.

17

Hear our stories: take heed.
We watch, and the foul, creeping creatures
of the darkness watch too.
They were watching *us.*

AGAINST INDOLENCE

At the height of summer, villagers would choose a human sacrifice for the pagan god Perun, to ensure crops remained safe from storms. The Polevik, one of Perun's demons, kept his eye on the fields, ready to punish any who shirked their labours for passing distractions.

A WORK PARTY of men was formed, travelling from farm to farm until all the harvest had been taken in. At one farm, a young wench was staying with her aunt and uncle, having been sent to learn how to milk the cows and tend to the chickens.

By late morning, she'd slip down to the fields to watch the men, admiring their muscled arms and strong torsos. The sight of their sweaty bodies awoke something inside her and she vowed that she'd sample them, each and every one, to discover what all the fuss was about.

She began with the man in charge, whispering her intention in his ear and then leading him to the edge of the field, where the rye still stood tall. He was more than willing, especially as she was a buxom maid, with a plump behind and a cheerful disposition.

With the prickle of dry stalks at her back, she opened her legs. His rough thrusts were just what she'd hoped for. Without inhibition or reservation, she complied with all the foreman's requests. Of him she requested nothing but the chance to sate her curiosity and, in return for the promise of a tumble each day, he agreed that she could take her pick of the other men and act as she chose.

Word spread quickly of the lascivious wench. The labourers, needless to say, had no objection to the plan.

After a few afternoons, in which she found out more about such matters than she could have foreseen, her field adventures began to lose their thrall. Finding the men hers to command, she enjoyed a sense of power, but felt the need for something more dangerous, more forbidden.

She lay languidly in the sun, skirts raised and fingers dabbling below, imagining her lovers watching her tender ministrations. No sooner had such thoughts entered her mind than she heard a low growl and sat up to see a dark figure of a man at her feet, looking into her most intimate of places.

He was broader than any other she'd known, with large strong hands, and hair curled thick down his neck. He licked his lips and his eyes left her in no doubt that she had taken his fancy.

He held the promise of mischief and that, as we know, can lead into territory most treacherous.

> Here, from the edges, we see indolence and
> vanity.

We know what feeds upon human folly.

Flinging her skirts down in a show of modesty, and rising with alacrity, she asked from whence he'd come.

'Innocent young maiden,' said he, with an undeniable smirk, 'I'm indeed a new face. I'm visiting my uncle in the next village and have come to join the harvesting party.' At which, he placed one of his huge hands over his groin and gave it a lecherous rub, in case his meaning might be unclear.

'What a coincidence,' she replied, averting her eyes in a coy fashion. 'I'm a visitor here, too. It's a delight to meet new people and discover new ways.'

'Ha hoi!' cried he, making ready to grab her waist. 'I may have new games to show you. Let's see what you're made of!'

'Not so fast,' the girl answered, jumping to one side. 'Dear Sir, we've only just met. I can hardly kiss a man to whom I've not been introduced. You're quite a stranger to me; it wouldn't be proper.'

A snarl rose in his throat and she felt a tremble of fear, knowing that she was at his mercy; the sensation was sweet indeed. She closed her eyes in anticipation but no assault occurred. Rather, he vanished.

Disappointed, she flounced home, her pride wounded, cursing him, yet secretly hoping that he'd appear again on the morrow.

All night, she wriggled in her little wooden cot, dreaming of hot hands and sharp teeth nipping her flesh; by morning, she was quite exhausted with desire.

She collected the hens' eggs with less care, and had no

inclination to soothe the cattle with lullabies as she milked; her mind was upon one thing only and, with each hour, her lust grew. That afternoon, she accepted several of the labourers greedily in succession. However, she could find no satisfaction and, as the day drew to a close, she beat her fists in the dirt, wild with vexation.

From behind, she heard a low chuckle. There he stood.

'Good afternoon, young maid. Have you been waiting for me?'

Defiant, she replied, 'Of course not. You didn't enter my head. I've been far too busy to think of you!'

At this, he laughed and clicked his tongue in reprimand.

'You can think of nothing but me and will have no rest until I've devoured you.'

His tongue moved across his teeth and they seemed to elongate as he did so. He sniffed the air and smiled. 'Do you taste as good as you smell?'

She could have sworn that, where his tongue had been, a small flame now flickered.

'We're no longer strangers, since we met yesterday, so that can hardly be an objection.'

She felt breathless with desire, but cast down her eyes demurely, telling him she could never romp with more than five men in an afternoon, and she'd already had her fill.

His eyes flashed in annoyance and, for a moment, she felt sure that one was yellow and the other green, where both had been common brown before. He grabbed her hair, so that she let out a yelp.

'Let me go,' she bleated, stamping on his foot. 'No one's having me unless I'm good and ready!'

He gave her hair another tug, then placed his mouth beside her ear. 'I'll meet you tomorrow at noon.'

She ran home without looking back and flung herself onto her narrow bed, sobbing with fright and excitement.

She tossed and turned, as the night before, able to think only of what new erotic delights might be revealed. She dreamt of the stranger chasing her through the fields, she and he naked both, and then into the forest dark. Closer he came, closer and closer. When her legs could bear no more she fell into the damp leaves, and he was upon her, eyes glinting. His mouth, so large, lowered between her legs and he sucked there, as she twisted, his tongue probing deep.

The next morning, she woke late, her body moist with sweat and pleasure.

Sitting later among the heavy-uddered cows, and pulling on their teats, her thoughts flitted most teasingly to what might await her. She vowed that, once she'd tried the stranger, she'd give up her saucy ways. She'd return to her village and pretend that she was a virgin – as if her antics of the past days had been a fantasy.

In her haste to return to their chosen spot, she left her pails in the middle of the milking parlour, where the cows might easily kick them over.

She passed the labourers with hardly a glance, but heard the harsh words of the head man, berating them for their thoughtlessness. Distracted by the romps of the previous day, they'd left the hay bales tied clumsily, so that the wind had blown them far and wide. The last good days of the summer were slipping away, and there was no time to be lost in gathering crops and winter fodder.

Tossing her head, for what mattered hay bales to her, she hurried to where her mysterious lover waited.

She saw at once, by the strength of his maypole, that he was ready to begin. There was no further benefit in playing games so she allowed him to guide her beneath a tree, where the shade was cool.

How long his nails were, soil-blackened and rather sharp.

Be careful with those,' she clucked. 'You might snag my blouse!' Then, playfully, she unlaced the garment and threw it over her head, letting her heavy bosom bounce free.

He ran a harsh nail down her breast, over its peak, and she gasped, for there is pleasure in pain. He then loosened her skirt and petticoats so that she might step free. She stood, plump and naked and a little bashful, which made her declare, 'Come on then, you cheeky beast. Do you have something for me or are you only here to look?'

At her command, he removed his shirt and trousers, revealing that which she had both anticipated and feared. He was surprisingly hairy.

Before she could utter a squeak, the Polevik lifted her several feet in the air, pushing her against the tree. She offered some objection, yet wrapped her legs around his waist, to draw him in more closely.

> You who crave illicit pleasures of the flesh,
> Beware.

Temptation can lead you on an ill-chosen
    path,
where may lurk foul fiends.

His hands he placed on either cheek, where there was plenty to grab hold of. With a squeeze, he asked, 'Am I not gallant enough for you? Shall I stop?'

She could only pant, 'No, no. Carry on.'

There was no coolness in the shade now; his skin burned hot.

If she had opened her eyes, she would have seen leering triumph in his. Then, in a manner less than gentlemanly, the Polevik shoved her to the ground, entering her from behind with indelicate force.

'Oi oi!' she protested. 'I'm not an animal in the field. You'll tear me in two if you carry on like that.'

She thought she might have made a mistake but, quicker than a snake through the grass, he withdrew that which offended her and gave her his tongue in its stead.

'Shall I stop?' he asked, flicking this way and that. His tongue felt forked, touching her in a way quite unfamiliar.

'No, no,' she gulped. 'It's really rather nice.'

Glancing back through her legs, she couldn't help but notice that he seemed hairier than ever.

The hands kneading her rump also felt more like paws, with claws scratching her flesh.

'Careful back there,' she reminded him.

The field devil pushed further with its tongue and sucked hard.

'But don't stop,' she whispered.

With a snort and a whoop, the Polevik opened its

mouth wide and took a large bite, followed by several more. He gobbled her up until nothing more remained – and a juicy meal she was.

When nothing more remained, he almost felt regret: to remove such a lusty young woman from the world was a shame indeed. However, she had been idle in her duties and had distracted the labourers from theirs.

In her absence, the workers resumed their former focus. In fact, their cheerfully saucy memories of the wench made them work all the harder, as they threshed the grain.

It was a very good harvest that year.

AGAINST DECEIT

*Some wives are cursed with men who drink too much; others
have gamblers for husbands, or womanisers, or those with
heavy hands. Some wed brutes committed to all these vices. Of
course, a good many husbands are upright men, who take no
pleasure in excess, deceit or violence, however shrewish their
wives.*

*We have no need to peek at keyholes; all life is ours to witness.
Moreover, we see not only the obvious, but the inner thoughts of
men and women which, as you know, are often at variance with
what their mouths utter.*

Here, at the edges, we see what you cannot.

THERE WAS ONCE a woman whose husband, a farmer of
goats, was considerate in all things, so that she had
nothing of which to complain. His only fault was that he
was exceptionally dull.

In contrast, his wife had an unflagging appetite for
excitement.

As is so often the way, her eyes fell upon their handsome neighbour: the owner of a good herd of cows. She would linger at the gate, hoping to catch a glimpse of him about his work.

In church, her thoughts strayed from matters divine to those shamefully carnal, relishing imaginings of future sins. Kneeling within her pew to pray, her fingers would creep beneath her skirts, to dip and dally where they should not.

As with all desires left unfulfilled and forbidden in nature, time fuelled the furnace, so that her lust for the man grew out of all proportion.

Such is humankind's weakness; as we, the damned spirits of the hereafter, know so well. There is no vice with which we are unfamiliar.

> Here, from the edges,
> between light and shade,
> We spy on man's folly:
> that ever-unrolling tapestry,
> daily embroidered anew.

At last, unable to control her impulses, the hussy accosted him in his milking shed.

'I've come to borrow buckets,' said she, but the strumpet placed her hand where none but his wife's should wander, and gave his sausage a squeeze.

So easy it is to capture a man's attention!

The object of her rapture was more than compliant, but his goodly spouse was within a spit, feeding the chickens in the yard.

To her chagrin, the wench was obliged to contain her saucy enthusiasm. However, such determination as hers being not easily beaten and ardour fanning the flames of invention, she promised him more pleasures if he would follow her direction.

The wily woman persuaded her husband, much against his natural inclination, to invite their neighbour for a friendly game of dice. Knowing that he had no tolerance for drink above a rare glass of beer, she arranged that all would be against him.

The evening proceeded as she had foreseen, with her poor husband losing all his coin. Into his beer, she had poured a measure of potent *samogon,* so that his judgement was greatly impaired.

When he had also staked and lost seven of their finest nanny goats, he fell upon his knees, asking if he might settle the obligation in some other fashion.

At this, the neighbour made a request. As counselled by the strumpet wife, he asked if he might visit every evening for a week, for a single hour.

Then, he bent close to the husband's ear and whispered a terrible admission. 'In truth,' declared he, 'and to my shame, I have little idea of how to please a woman.'

Praising the goat farmer's contented marriage, he voiced his hope that the man's wife might share her most intimate of secrets. 'In teaching me the true desires of an honest woman's heart,' beseeched the cad, 'she might help me to enjoy a measure of your marital bliss.'

Being a gentle soul, with much compassion, the good husband felt sympathy. Moreover, he was flattered by the words of his companion, and made bold by the alcohol in his veins. He drew his wife aside to ask if she might agree to the arrangement.

Of course, she feigned scorn and indignation at the notion but, before her hapless spouse could beseech her forgiveness, she vowed that she held her duty to obey above all else.

'I would never refuse your request, dearest husband,' she vowed, 'However onerous…'

Naturally, the harlot was delighted that her plan had succeeded.

So it is that lust, and the temptation of what is forbidden, leads us into mischief.

The next night, the neighbour paid the first of his visits, telling his own wife that he yearned for an hour of masculine company and conversation.

Adultery is a sin most heinous – and yet, how willingly our flesh succumbs.

The sly lovers frolicked uninterrupted, the neighbour proving himself, to the hussy's delight, highly skilled in the bedroom. So great was his talent that the strumpet congratulated herself most heartily on her deceit.

Upon the second evening, the lewd grunts of the incorrigible pair caught the sharp ears of a prowling demon, bringing it beneath the very window. It watched hungrily, seeing all too well what was afoot.

And we, in the shadows, watched too.

Such creatures are not reputed for their sense of justice, but they do claim the villainous for their own, so the beast had no compunction in teaching the lecherous pair a lesson.

The next evening, the fiend cast a spell of sleep over

the philandering neighbour and, donning his cloak, arrived in his place. The husband barely looked upon him, so miserable and ashamed was he at having entered into the contract.

The demon found the wife in the dimly lit bedroom, welcoming her caller with lewd suggestions. The beast laughed darkly upon hearing her unseemly requests.

'Good lady,' it crooned, 'I promise to do my best to satisfy you.' Throwing off the cloak, it allowed the woman to see what awaited her and, before she could scream, stoppered her voice with its hairy fist. Being powerless to escape the creature's grasp, she had no choice but to allow it to enjoy her in every fashion.

Having had its fill, the brute warned her that it would take the place of her lover on all future occasions, should she feel inclined to continue her lascivious ways. Filled not only with humiliation but abject fear, the deceitful wife promised with all haste to mend her ways.

Much to the neighbour's frustration, the chastened woman forbade him to visit any more. She never bothered him again and thenceforward kept her thoughts firmly on her prayers each Sunday.

Meanwhile, the husband rebuked himself for having fallen into dissolute ways, swearing never to gamble or drink again. He begged his wife's clemency for having subjected her to such indignity and vowed to lavish her with greater attention from that day forward. Realising that the man she'd married was worthy more of regard than mockery, she promised also to be faithful and true, attending more closely to his comforts.

The demon's hateful ravishment thus brought about

some improvement in their married state, and ensured the contentment of the couple for many years to come.

Whenever the moon hung large and cool, the devilish creature would return to that window to sniff the air, but never again did it find cause to lift the curtain.

GLOSSARY

Samogon: a strongly alcoholic drink distilled from fermented potatoes and beets, with herbs and juniper often added (similar to vodka).

AGAINST ENVY

IN A PLACE KNOWN for its fields of shimmering buckwheat lived two children inseparable; twin sisters, born under the same celestial sky, divided by only a few minutes in taking their first breath. Still damp from the womb, their tiny fingers clutched one to the other.

They shared not only their meals but their games and their clothes – even their hairbrush and soap. Secrets there were none, as they whispered beneath the sheets. They wriggled their feet together, in nightly embraces against the cold.

Until, once day, with the tickle of the wind, or the passing of a malign force, the maidens' parents were taken from this world and sent to the next. Perhaps it was just as Fate had always intended.

Human hearts are unfathomable in their grief, in their wants and whims. Who knows what drives us this way or that?

We who are beyond the mortal world see many things

from the edges; we hear the subtle shifts of rhythm in the beat of a blackening heart.

Circumstance, or nature, brought about a change between the sisters.

Svetlana and Anya were identical in looks but, while one's nature grew daily to resemble that of a dove, her open heart filled with kindness and love, her sibling began ever more to keep her thoughts and desires close hidden.

Like a snake, Anya learnt to charm others with flattery and deceit, while concealing her true thoughts, selfish and cruel.

As the years passed, discontent etched at the corners of her mouth and a hard glint settled in her eye.

Their grandmother, who now had the care of them, felt unease, as she noted the growing differences between the two sisters. With eyes ever drawn to the darkness in human souls, we watched too, and one sister more closely than the other.

The old lady did her best to divide her love equally between the two young women, and to guide both towards contentment. Yet, she saw Anya's nature, and her anxiety kept her awake long after blowing out her evening candle.

THE SEASONS CYCLED as they must, with the buckwheat growing tall and golden, until ripe for gathering. Once the harvest was safely stacked and covered, the village folk turned their minds to matchmaking, hosting evening dances for young maidens and lads, in order that pairs might be struck, under the watchful eye of the village elders. So it was that the grandmother helped the girls tie bright ribbons in their hair and dotted their lips red with beetroot juice, kissing them tenderly as they set off for evenings of song and merriment.

Svetlana's purity brought her many suitors, and she came to rest in the arms of a lad equally innocent in mind and spirit. The handsome couple's devotion and joy inspired others to find matches. Soon, all but a handful were formally betrothed – the disdainful serpent sister among those who looked on with envy.

The slow maggot-rot of jealousy ate at Anya's heart, as the day of her sister's wedding approached ever closer, and she began contemplating ways to end the couple's happiness.

> Ambition, envy and greed;
> We know what you covet.

Her first thought was to cause her sister's beauty to wither. One night, from within the long-shared intimacy of their bed, she cut the ties that bound them along with a lock of Svetlana's hair.

This lock she coated in soil and hung inside the chimney, uttering words of malice; as the dirt dried, the spell would cause her sister's skin to shrivel like that of an ancient crone.

However, a little mouse, watching over the girl, carried the lock of hair between its teeth and dropped it in a nearby stream, so that it might never dry out.

As the days passed, the sweet-tempered maiden grew

only more beautiful, alongside her love for her betrothed, while her sibling's hatred grew ever stronger.

It came time for the married women of the village to bake the wedding loaf: the *karavai*. Bestowed with blessings, it would bring fair fortune to the newlyweds. The wicked girl watched through a window as the *karavanitsas* kneaded the dough across their wooden table.

As they worked, they urged the dough to rise and be flavoursome. However, despite two of their number being auspiciously pregnant and not a bad-word spoken, the mixture refused to bind. The women toasted it with potato vodka, pouring a libation of *samogon* into its centre, but still it stuck stubbornly to the table and emitted a foul smell.

'Never was there such a true match. How can the loaf be so capricious?' cried one.

To which the dough replied, 'Evil thoughts are abroad. I'll grace no wedding feast.'

The women fled in terror, abandoning the loaf.

No one caught sight of the serpent girl at the window, whose scowl had turned to glee on hearing the words of ill-omen.

Despite their fear, the *karavanitsas* pledged to keep secret what had happened, and substitute another loaf when the time came, so fond were they of the young couple, whose love became more apparent with each passing day.

On the eve of the wedding, when dusk had fallen, the gentle girl's friends wrapped their most brightly coloured shawls about them and came to collect her for the bridal bath. They jostled to escort her, clasping her by the waist and tripping over their own feet in anticipation of girlish gossip.

The village *banya* was decorated for the occasion, filled with sweet wild mint, denoting the bride's virginity. There, they took turns washing her hair and stroking her back with damp cloths of linen. They kissed her shoulders, whispering good wishes in her ear: for everlasting love, for a happy home and for plump, laughing babies.

When her loose-flowing tresses were dry, they combed a hundred strokes. Later, they would plait her hair and wind the braid close around her head, to indicate her transformation from maiden to wife.

The serpent sister looked on in malcontent, hot loathing simmering within her breast. So rapt were the young women in their skittish talk, contemplating the pleasures of the marital bed, that none noticed her sneer.

> And what you covet
> Draws dark forces ever nearer.

Able to endure no more, Anya reminded them that the water used in washing the bride should now be wrung out from their little cloths and collected in a jug. She would take it to the groom for his ritual drinking.

This the girls did and the sister departed, hiding behind some blackberry bushes to drink the magical water. While it would cast a spell of eternal adoration over the bride's true love, on any other it would bestow, temporarily, her radiant vitality.

Anya stayed concealed until all had returned to their homes, then crept back within the *banya* and quickly washed herself, pouring her own used water at last into the jug.

The magical potion had softened her features and scented her skin with the very smell of her dove-sister. When she tapped at the bedroom shutters of the young groom, half hidden by the shadows, he fell immediately under her thrall. Although he had not expected his beloved to deliver the *banya* water herself, so enflamed with love was he that he only too readily accepted her appearance.

'Let me in my love,' urged the serpent-girl, mimicking the soft voice of her sister. 'We're almost wed so surely there can be no harm.'

She stroked his cheek and blew lightly against his eyelids with her bewitching breath. There, in the gloom, she offered him the jug of her own bath water, ensuring that he drank deeply. Then, she pressed her mouth to his.

The lad's eyes became heavy with lust as the temptress entwined her arms about him and guided him to the floor. He buried his face in her neck, smelling there the familiar lilac scent of his maiden-pure, thinking only of her as his hands moved across Anya's breasts and hips.

'Oh my darling, true love,' he cried, as she parted her thighs.

The lad succumbed to her, until she possessed him, mind and body.

Then, all was done.

Her eyes shone in malicious delight as she slunk back to her bed, where her sister slumbered, dreaming of love.

Emboldened by her success, the serpent-girl sprinkled

belladonna onto her sister's lips, gathered from deadly nightshade in the woods.

The shadows watched her, as did the ancient oak from which the bed had been carved. The blanket upon the bed, spun and woven by their mother, watched too. A spider spinning in its web watched her with all of its eyes. And the ever-vigilant mice peeped through the chinks in the floorboards. All bore witness to her wicked misdeeds, and we, at the edges, watched through their eyes.

As dawn broke, fingers of light revealed the pale corpse upon the bed, flesh drained of all warmth: lips once ripe, mottled blue, and the rose-hue of her cheek now livid.

Deceitful and cunning, Anya let out a scream, her eyes full of tears, thanks to salt rubbed about them. The house soon filled with neighbours, weeping in condolence with the girls' grandmother. They worried that the poor woman's heart would break, so great was her grief.

The serpent within the wicked sister stretched and shivered in satisfaction. She slithered away, letting those weeping mourn and wail, showing just enough distress to avert their gaze.

She waited.

The young groom wept over the dove-maiden's corpse, clutching her pale hand in his, refusing to be parted from his Beloved. Hot tears of anger flowed at the unfair hand of Fate.

However, as the hours and days passed, he found

himself distracted by the sister he had barely noticed before. In her face, he saw the echo of his bride: no hardness or venom, only a familiar softness.

She cast crafty words of comfort, which curled into his heart, and lowered her eyes demurely when he drew close. Before long, he could not ignore the hunger she inspired in him. Convinced that he had been blessed with a second chance at love, he asked for her hand.

So relieved were the villagers to see the young man restored to himself that few spoke against the match and the wedding was held as soon as propriety would allow. The bride climbed onto her groom's cart to set off for church, wearing her red *sarafan*, her face veiled. Beneath, her smile was triumphant.

> We know the secrets of nature
> and of human hearts.
> We know what lies beneath,
> In the hidden corners of your soul.

The ceremony passed without event, his own mother's ring placed upon her finger. And so they were wed.

After the feast, at which the pair were treated as prince and princess, neither being allowed to lift even a hand to feed themselves, the guests carried them to their sleeping chamber, although with less mirth and banter than was usual on such occasions.

The fire, which had been lit earlier in the day to take the chill from the room, was extinguished, leaving a single candle, required to burn throughout that first night, in order to watch over the lovers.

> We are behind the door,
> in the corners,
> In the room where you've just
> extinguished the light.

Shrugging off their wedding attire, the pair wriggled beneath the covers, eager to warm one another. For a fleeting moment, the snake-sister recalled she who had so recently shared her bed; she whose little toes had pressed against hers as they whispered their secrets.

At her husband's first caress, the bride felt a cold touch upon her shoulder. She turned abruptly in surprise, but the room was empty.

> And we're not alone; not alone
> Here in the dark.

'I'm sorry my love,' her groom answered. Thinking that his own hands must be chill, he blew on them, then moved further under the sheets, kissing her belly.

The candlelight threw strange shadows, as if the corners of the room were alive, so she closed her eyes, wishing to feel completely alone with her new husband.

In truth, the room was quite crowded. We watched, and the hungry dark things lurked, and alongside, pale and grief-stricken, the dove-sister watched too, taking her place among us, the restless dead.

Anya sighed as her husband's hot breath travelled lower but her gasp of pleasure turned to fright as she felt a sharp tug at her hair.

'My darling one; don't be afraid,' soothed her groom, hidden below the blankets. 'I won't hurt you.'

Eyes wide in terror, she watched as the shades climbed the walls and took shape, with fangs and clapper-claws, ready to bite. Scaly fingers wove into her hair, tugging with spite. Nippers snipped and pincers clipped, plucking at her nose. Talons snatched and shredded and sliced.

She drummed her feet against the mattress, but her scream died in her throat.

'My wonderful wild one,' murmured her husband, holding her all the more ardently from under the covers. She could barely move.

Unrelenting eyes gleamed. She heard a hiss in her ear.

'We watch, we wait, we never forget. Black hearts beget black ends.'

The shadows fell upon her and whisked her away, into dark and relentless torment, in that place set aside for deceivers such as she.

Her groom they left, in an empty bed, with nothing but the echo of a gentle caress upon his cheek, and the scent of lilac upon his pillow.

GLOSSARY

Banya: an outside bath-house, used as a sauna, with an ante-room often used for disrobing. Not only a place for washing, it is thought to have its own powers, being once used as a place of birthing and for ritualistic cleansing, such as on the night before a wedding.

Karavai: the wedding loaf, large and round, decorated with dough birds and flowers. Tugged into two during the marriage ceremony by the bride and groom. Whoever possesses the larger share will 'rule' the home.

Karavanitsas: those who bake the wedding loaf.

Sarafan: a full skirted, long pinafore dress, often embroidered, under which a blouse is worn.

AGAINST MISERLINESS

A CERTAIN YOUNG girl had such skill in making pies and bread that she earned a reputation far and wide. Few could resist the aroma of her fresh, soft rolls and her succulent *pirozhki* pastries.

Men returning from the fields, or from business in town, would often follow their noses to her door. So, despite being stout of figure, and with teeth already decaying from indulgence in jam tarts, her talents as a cook brought her many suitors.

Thinking to serve the girl's interests, her parents selected for her the wealthiest of all those who came calling: an elderly widower who owned a large farm.

Her new husband was not unkind but he was miserly. Despite his fortune, he was reluctant to hire others to perform the dirty business of the house. The cheapskate commanded his young wife to undertake a great many duties: washing clothes and linens, scrubbing floors and windows, feeding the chickens and other livestock, milking the goats and cows, tending the vegetable patch, grooming his horse, and keeping the cobwebs from gathering. She would find his sharp elbows poking into her ribs whenever he caught her slacking.

In addition, he commanded her to cook him three fine meals every day. He would request all manner of elaborate recipes, gleeful at keeping her busy.

Of course, now that the wily gentleman had a bride to work her fingers to the bone, his coins could remain in his wooden chest, under lock and key.

Meanwhile, his son from his first marriage undertook the rougher labours of the estate, aided by three men-of-work.

Hoping to soften his heart and allow her to bring in help, she prepared her finest delicacies for her husband. Moreover, she uttered not a word of rebuke when he asked her to wash his bunion-covered feet, or to clip his crusted, yellow toenails.

The girl's physical needs were met in every respect: except one. On laying his head on the pillow, the dry old stick would fall unconscious, never thinking that she might require his attention.

Each night, she was forced to endure her husband's grunts, but only as he passed wind during his gluttonous fits of sleep, rather than in passion.

He noticed not when she wore a newly embroidered nightgown or placed an encouraging hand upon his back. He had not married her for the issue of children, having a grown son already.

It was not what she had hoped for and the poor girl grew despondent. One morning, having emptied the contents of her husband's chamber pot, and scrubbed his undergarments vigorously on her wash-board, she set her mind on seeking what she lacked.

The man's son was not the most handsome, having eyes slightly crossed and teeth more than commonly crooked, but his shoulders were broad and his body hard and lean, thanks to his daily labouring.

Moreover, he was young and fit and she had felt his eyes linger upon more than her pies: a fact neither escaping her aged spouse.

Of course, in the dark, a handsome face matters less than a strong hand and a determined staff. She thought, *'He'll do for me.'*

Waiting until her husband was snoring, she crept to the bed of his son and offered him warm delights through the early hours. With ready blood in his veins and no wife of his own, he was more than happy to satisfy her requests. In fact, the arrangement suited them both perfectly.

The young wench was quite a saucy piece, such that, forgetting herself, she allowed her robust moans of pleasure to rouse her husband, who awoke to an empty bed.

Jumping up quicker than his old bones found comfortable, he ran to his son's room and set about searching for the trollop. He found nothing, since the girl had hidden herself well, at the back of the wardrobe, and her husband's eyes were not what they once were.

The old codger returned to his warm covers, convinced that something lewd was afoot. The girl was not without wit so she crept to the kitchen, returning to her marital bed with a few morsels.

Her husband at once confronted her with his suspicions and she was obliged to admit that she had been indulging her appetite: eating savouries in the kitchen. Such was her enjoyment that she had cried out in pleasure. In her napkin were *pirozhki* she had made that morning for him to try.

The meat and cabbage pies held a mouth-watering gravy and were tasty indeed. She kissed him tenderly on the forehead and promised to make the same recipe for him the next day.

Having risked discovery, the lovers were forced to put aside their games. However, their hunger for one another could not be denied. Eventually, the young man suggested that they meet in the barn, where her cries would not be so easily heard. The wench had little taste for frolicking in the animals' hay, but the weather had become warmer and she was eager to resume her nightly frolics.

The son suggested that they wait until past the hour of midnight, so that his father would be soundly asleep, and would not notice her absence. At this, the girl despaired, believing that she would fail to wake at the appropriate time.

With great inventiveness, her beau directed her to tie a piece of string to her toe and hang it out between the shutters. He would wake her with a tug and, the room being situated at ground level, she might slip easily from the window.

On blowing out the candle, the hussy waited until she heard her husband's snores. She then tied the string as she had been told, left the window ajar, and awoke later to the signal.

The couple passed several hours in mutual delight,

until the cockerel brought in the dawn and the girl slipped back to her bed.

Months passed and the old skinflint, while still wary of his wife's faithfulness, could find nothing with which to reproach her. In fact, she appeared more content than ever, despite her heavy workload, singing as she baked delicious dishes for him. He only wondered if perhaps she might be sampling too much of her own cooking, since her belly was clearly growing from so much indulgence.

It so happened that, one night, a spider dropped down on its silken thread, landing on the old man's nose and waking him with its tickling. Feeling a draught from the window, he rose to close it and there saw the string, so artfully employed. Finding it tied to the toe of his wife, he unfastened the loop and, returning to the bed, placed it about his own, awaiting whatever might happen.

Before long, he felt a tug and awoke. The yanking upon the string was of such violence that the miser was made to hop across the room in quite ridiculous fashion; there was no doubt in his mind that he'd find his wife's lover upon the other end.

As Fate, or the strange ways of nature, would have it, that night, a cave-demon had recently woken from its long, winter sleep. Its underground lair was a comfortable home, with a fresh spring and a family of bats, convenient for sating its appetite. On this very evening, the creature had taken a fancy to sample the air and see what might be afoot.

Its meanderings took it to the miser's farm, perhaps to find a chicken or goat or cow left unguarded. There, it came upon the string, so beguilingly placed.

What should it do but tug upon it?

The old man was incensed, ready to cudgel the head of whomever he met at the tail end of the string. Throwing open the shutters, a great jerk pulled him clean off his feet, through the air, and into the arms of the curious beast.

Having lived so much in the dark, the demon's sight, like that of the old stick, was very poor. Feeling the modest weight of the body in its arms and smelling the fresh floral scent of the moneygrubber's nightshirt, so carefully laundered, the creature assumed that a ripe young maiden had fallen upon him.

'Ahh! My pretty one,' cooed the fiend, its slender claws stroking the old man's few locks of hair. 'What delights have you under your flimsy attire?'

The creature reached under the fabric and began to tickle the aged skinflint. Struck dumb with horror, he pushed the talons away as best he could, but the action only made the foul fiend chuckle.

'You coy young thing,' it purred. 'We'll soon cure you of that.'

Aroused by the struggles of its prey, the demon bent the man over and fumbled beneath his nightgown, grasping at the miser's bony buttocks, until it discovered treasures unexpected.

'Never mind,' snorted the beast. 'Nobody's perfect.'

Without further ado, it plunged its demon-staff between the old codger's cheeks, holding a furry paw to stop its plaything's mouth. Only the faintest of squeaks was audible as the fiend had its way, mounting the miser with voracious enthusiasm.

Thus plays out the balance of good and evil, sin punished when least expected: retribution arriving in unexpected form. Perhaps, demons are as powerless to resist the guiding hand of Fate, and of their nature, as we poor souls are helpless in succumbing to ours.

So pleased was the creature with its new pet that it carried the pinchfist back to its cave, to keep him company in the long hours of darkness.

The miser, of course, was never seen again, leaving the young wife to marry her ardent and devoted sweetheart.

Her eager hands were no more required to scrub floors, making plenty of time to pinch the cheeks of their baby daughter, who was born with the most contented disposition, and who never wanted for a dainty morsel of cabbage pie.

AGAINST BLIND RIVALRY

As a snake would shed its skin, Kaliady is a time of new beginnings. Revellers don animal masks, particularly those of a goat's head, to sing from house to house. They share good wishes for the New Year, and beg korovki pastries. It is a time of tricks and mischief, dancing and revelry, as well as fortune-telling for what lies ahead.

HERE IS a tale of concealment and secrets, of lust and rivalry, of fresh snow, waiting for a certain footstep. Here is *Kaliady* night, with fires lit to drive out not just the chill but other shades of darkness, which are ever at the edges, waiting and watching. Draw close now, closer to the hearth.

There may lurk creatures wily, demon tricksters, intent on mischief and deceit, for their own pleasure. Demons so often wear humanity's blemished traits; they sit so well upon their deceitful pelts.

You think you tell the stories, but the hearth helps you remember. The flames have memories too. Family after family have gathered, generation after generation, recounting their stories. The flames have heard much. And we, flickering in the flames, we remember what you care to forget.

We remember the old ways, we know they have wisdom.

Gather round. Draw closer, and listen well. Not just with your ears, but with your eyes and your lips, your skin and your blood.

Such nights as this are made for storytelling, when lakes are ice-locked and forests snow-blanketed deep, prowled by hunter-wolves. They are made for stolen kisses, for lovers' arms wrapped against the frost, under starlit skies. They are made for pulse-seeking predators, and the sweet thrill of anticipation. It is late. The young men have enjoyed their romps and buffoonery. Now, bellies full, they're dozing deep, befuddled with drink.

THE GIRLS HAD GONE their own way, to a barn at one end of the village, to light candles and cast feminine spells, as only women can when they gather together: to summon their future, calling visions of husbands to their dreams.

The breath of those ardent yearnings blew sweetly into our realm. Even here, in the dark, such honeyed hungers can be felt, so potently do they call.

They danced a khorovod and sang:

> Send us a bull,
> A bull with big horns.

They twirled in their circle, clapping their hands.

> Send us a wolf,
> A wolf with sharp teeth.

They sang with intent, imagining rough paws.

> Send us a suitor, a husband, a swain,
> A lover to warm the blood in our veins.

On nights such as this, words summon not only human lovers but all those who hunt. At the barn door there appeared one with the face of a goat, his figure broad and tall. He watched them for a while, unnoticed, and then stepped forward, causing a pause in their frolics.

'Girls only here!' reprimanded one.

'Who's this then?' asked another. 'Is it you Ivan? With your great hands? Or is it Sergei the forester? Only he has such red hair! Take off your mask and let us see!' There was much teasing and titters; it was time for some fun.

'I may be one you know, or perhaps you know me not,' replied he, voice slick with mischief. 'You're looking for husbands I see. What matters my face? Will any take me to their bed?'

There was something in the way that voice stroked their skin, and whispered to their loins that held the girls' attention, as if he were the only man worthy of their desire, and they must be the one to have him.

Of course, no woman likes to lose a man's attention to her neighbour, and here was a specimen more than worthy of attainment. At once, they began arguing.

The goat-masked man, manipulative creature that he was, delighted to hear this girlish bickering.

'There is only one way to decide, my gentle maidens,' he announced, at last. 'In choosing my wife, I must glimpse your beast within. Let it awaken and snap its jaws.'

At this, he dropped his trousers, to reveal a manhood shocking in proportion. Beneath hung huge testicles, bristled vivid ginger.

Being country girls, they'd all seen a man's assets before, and most had done a great deal more than look. However, this generous endowment was unexpected.

Now, each had but one wish: to prove herself the most wanton and alluring.

> You who crave illicit pleasures of the flesh,
> Beware...

Such thoughts are easily perceived by demon-beasts (as such this was, summoned by the girls' lustful ardour). How easy it is for evil forces to work upon a woman's vanity, and her competitive nature. The creature laughed in amusement at the predictability of human rivalry.

'Ladies, let's not waste a minute,' it declared, clapping its hands in glee. 'Form a circle, facing away. I'll have my way with each in turn, and I promise marriage to she who most pleases me. I'll keep on my mask so that, if anyone is tempted to peep over her shoulder, she won't be able to read my expression. It would pain me to see any of you disheartened, should my face betray any emotion less than delight.'

Of course, such words only steeled the girls in their determination to outperform their village-sisters.

They formed a circle and, one by one, turned outwards, hearts pounding, excited fingers grasping their skirts. Who, oh who, would he choose first?

Silently, they all wondered to themselves: how best to show passion? How should a woman show her inner wolf, enticing a man's lust?

The mystery guest surveyed the circle of inviting rumps. He'd sample them all, but where to begin?

Here was one, skirts raised the highest, and bending over eagerly. Pretending to adjust her garter, he could just glimpse her cunt dew-slick: plump pillows waiting for his head. Hands upon her ample hips, the demon nudged its nose between her cheeks, and snuffled at her mackerel slit.

'Fish for feasting,' it declared, and began its supper, breath hot upon those fleshy gates.

'On my grandmother's teeth!' cried out the girl.

The creature's agile tongue slid within. And what a tongue! As thick as a man's member and so very long, each delving slurp near knocked her off her feet.

The others, in their curiosity, could not help but spy and the sight caused them some alarm.

The demon lover suckled so hard at that milky fountain that the maid became dizzy with desire.

'Quick about it!' she shouted at last. 'I can wait no longer! Fuck me now. I'm good and ready.'

Ploughed and watered by every young man who took her fancy, she was far from chaste, and had no compunction about demanding her fill.

With a bark of satisfaction, the goat-beast made rude entry, spearing her roughly with its cudgel. It bounced her then upon its lap, giving a mighty roar.

'Eeeek!' cried she, and fell half into faint. No mortal man had ever doused her so. Those either side held her up, exchanging looks of consternation.

'Ha!' hooted the creature. 'We've just begun, my ladies lovely. I won't keep you waiting long.'

One might have thought the demon would be sated but its pole remained thick and primed. The girls' necks were quite cricked with turning so about.

The next gathered her petticoats and parted her thighs, half fearful, yet expectant.

Once more, the goat-fiend buried its muzzle deep, guzzling at potent juices. Its prickly beard scratched her soft skin, while its tongue, so deft, left her swooning. Curling into every crevice, it drank her salt-sweet syrup.

Her tufted lover gave her then a noisy smack upon the arse, and plunged itself full hilt.

A sexual waft met the noses of all: an aroma guaranteed to inspire!

'Oi Oi Oi!' she bellowed, then fell to moaning with each thrust. She'd never felt such pleasure.

The demon busied itself with every girl, enjoying those female exclamations of delight. Some squirmed upon its rod; some squeaked; others shrieked.

So intent was their mysterious lover upon pleasing them that they almost forgot the competition, of proving themselves the most willing of partners.

Each cunt kissed was rendered slippery with desire, ready to receive what nudged behind. Fuelled by the seed of those heavy testicles, the demon's organ was inde-fatigable.

At last, having licked and sucked and serviced all, with barely a drawing of breath between, the demon bowed low. It announced, 'Congratulations ladies dear! Exemplary are you all, and all will make good wives. I cannot choose, since all are so fine. I fear I must remain single, being unable to select my mate but, I promise that all will wed before the harvest of this coming year.'

And, to their great dismay, the fiend took to its tail.

AS FORETOLD, each maiden was courted, and married by spring. Never did they mention to their menfolk the liberties taken that *Kaliady* night and were left wondering, ever after, which had so seduced them.

Strangely enough, there were a great many early babies that year, each sprouting ginger curls. Meanwhile, no man wed had cause to think his marriage bed mundane. The demon lover, in taking advantage of the girls' vanity, unmasked their inner zeal. It ensured marriages of long contentment.

Every now and then, on the darkest of winter nights, as they performed their wifely duties, those brides might hear a lascivious laugh, from the corner, where the shadows sat thickest. Then, they could not help but ponder on the identity of their mysterious *Kaliady* lover, and whether he had been a man at all.

Such nights as this are made for storytelling. You think you tell the stories but the hearth helps you remember. The flames have memories too.

Remember the old ways.

Glossary

Kaliady: a pagan celebration of the end of year. The name may come from the Latin 'Calendae' or the word 'Kola' (wheel) - relating to the turn of the year. 'Yule' is an Anglo-Saxon word for wheel.

Korovki: pastries shaped as cows or goats for the festive season

Khorovod: a combination of a traditional circle dancing and chorus singing.

AGAINST PROLONGING THE
TORMENT OF GRIEF

BEYOND THE DEEPEST swathes of fir-dark forest, within the isolated Pripyat Marshes, two babes were born in neighbouring houses on the same night: a boy and a girl.

In that land of narrow waterways, tiny island villages and claggy peat bogs, they grew up almost as brother and sister, their mothers being as close as can be. Between mossy banks and water-waders, they swam in lakes and streams, made pipes from reeds and swung in tree branches. In mellow months, they fished for perch, pike and eel with cages and lines, in quiet contentment.

As the boy grew, he became the bravest of young men: broad-shouldered and noble, with hands turned only to good deeds. His fine looks were matched by those of his sweetheart, with her tresses golden. Their souls were woven from the same flax and embroidered from the same meadow: ever in harmony. The seasons changed the trees, but their love endured.

On balmy days, he would lay his head in her lap, so

that she might stroke his curls, and sing him into a blissful reverie.

Through the winter, she spun the finest wool, weaving her hopes into the cloth. She embroidered it richly with cornflowers and made him a jacket, taking care over every twist of the needle.

By the time their formal betrothal had been announced, it was clear that a child was surely on the way.

As the day approached for their marriage vows to be taken, the pair wrapped warmly and went to fish on the lake, where the ice had newly thawed. Pushing out their boat through the silt and rushes, they sat beneath the wide sky and frost-laced birches half-hidden in the haze.

It was from the depths of that chilly mist, hovering over the surface of the still and silent water, that we watched. In their seclusion, even the birds sounded remote, somewhere beyond.

> Beyond this world, evermore.
> Beyond life, yet not quite in death,
> Watching, watching,
> from the edges.

We watched as they shared kisses and the lad wrapped his arms around his beloved's shoulders, taking her mitten-clad hands between his.

As the boy began to punt them ashore, the weeds took his pole and, losing his balance, he tumbled in. The lake was cold but the lad was young and fit, and he often took a winter dip.

The girl hastily reached out her arm to help and, in

that moment, overturned the little boat. Sharp fingers of water slipped down her throat, causing a heavy languor to fall over her body.

The lad swam to the shore, pulling his love beside him, to hoist her upon the frost-hardened bank. Had he closed his eyes, everlasting slumber would have claimed them both, but he steeled his resolve, and heaved her across his shoulder. Leaning into the icy wind, with his clothes freezing on his back, he pushed on, step by step, though each stride drained the strength from his limbs, and chilled the marrow of his bones.

BY THE TIME SHE AWOKE, a fever held him in some unreachable place, between this life and the next. He walked dazed amidst us, in our tormented realm, where we, restless spirits, writhe and moan, bewailing our unfortunate imprisonment.

> We are the voices in the shadows,
> Between the light and shade,
> Betwixt life and restful death.

She kept vigil through the dark hours of night and the endless span of day, pressing the coolness of her hand against his burning forehead, and resting his fingers against her swollen belly.

On the fourth day, he seemed to revive and, helped by his mother, she spooned some soup to his lips, though they refused to swallow. In despair, she succumbed to tears and the bowl fell to the floor.

The dog leapt forward to lick the tasty broth but, on smelling the stew, turned its head away: a sign that the boy would soon pass into the next world, to join us in our anguish.

Sure enough, within the hour, the last breath escaped his body. Death's claw reached from the shadows and plucked him away.

His joy and laughter had been hers. Now, she desired only to sleep and never wake. How could he, so full of life and love, be forever lost to her? Her grief trapped her between silence and the eternal, furious wail of her broken heart.

His mother joined the girl in washing the tender corpse, dressing him in his best shirt and breeches, and his jacket of cornflowers, made with such love.

The menfolk laid him out and struck a small hole in the thatch of the roof, so that his soul might easily find its way. Water, bread and honey they placed on the windowsill, to sustain his spirit until it had taken its leave.

All watched over him, offering laments for the loss of such a young soul, but none grieved as deeply as his bride.

We watched those falling tears, each one so precious. Were such tears shed for us? By those we left behind? For some they were, but not for all.

If all else had been taken from her, yet she would have breathed on, secure in his arms. Without him, life lay heavy: a burden too great. In losing him, she had become a stranger to the world and all in it.

His joy and laughter had been hers. Now, she desired only to sleep and never wake. How could he, so full of life and love, be forever lost to her?

Wrapped in deepening grief, her thoughts crept often to the lake, wishing that it might close her in its arms, offering the eternal embrace of death, and release her from suffering.

As dawn broke on the day chosen for his burial, she whispered her lament close to his ear, so that only he might hear:

> Spring winds cease and
> Time hold still.
> Death has kissed those lips,
> Once mine.
>
> Never will I forget thee,
> By day or evening's glow.
>
> Only when dust fills my eyes and
> Coffin boards cover my feeble frame,
> Will my mourning end.
>
> Sorrow sits beside my pillow.
> No rest shall I have
> until I sleep in the moist earth.

His coffin she lined with goose feathers, to create a soft bed, and they carried his body to the grave, knocking the box against the threshold three times so that he might bid farewell to his childhood home.

In the days following, her eyes were blind to the new blossoms unfurling and her skin felt only the cold embrace of loneliness, rather than the growing warmth of spring. No food passed her lips and no peaceful slumber came: only terrors of being lost in the dark, alone. Pain and sadness enveloped her like a damp shawl.

The desire to follow her groom into the Unknown became a daily temptation. Only the thought of the babe within stopped her.

One night, by the dim light of a crescent moon, she slipped from her restless bed, donning felt boots and coat to walk to the edge of the village, to the cemetery planted round with fir and yew.

She placed her head on the damp soil of her lover's grave, below the night's glitter. A breeze passed softly across the fringe of the long grass and carried her breath: a ghostly vapour in the still hours.

And then, a flame began to gleam, and another; lights unnatural.

She became at once aware of the sleepers around her in the hard earth, and grew fearful of their unquiet slumbers, as well she might.

Dark wings glided and came to rest on her true love's headstone. A crow, plumage glossy, gave its bead-black stare, and in those eyes she saw not the cold gaze of a bird, but the soul of her Beloved.

He had journeyed from the Beyond, where we dwell, to inhabit the bird and comfort his Beloved.

Its broken half-voice told her, 'Go home my love. Your heart beats while all here are cold in Death. The longer you stay, the closer to Death you will travel, your life draining into the very soil and into the lingering spirits. This is no place for the living.'

A star shot across the firmament, its light extinguishing as it reached the far curve of its arc. 'So it is,' she thought, stroking her rounded stomach. 'There are just as many stars in the sky as there are human beings on earth, a new star appearing whenever a babe is born, and another disappearing when someone dies. My love's light has gone and another awaits its birth.'

The flames dimmed and the crow stretched its wings to soar ahead, guiding her back to her own bed.

The bird's visit comforted the girl and, for several days, her heart lightened, knowing that the spirit of her Beloved watched over her.

> We are your lovers long gone,
> Whispering to you
> From the edges.

However, as time passed, she felt her grief even more keenly, dreaming now of his gentle touch and soft lips. In each shifting cloud she saw his image while the dusk became his tender caress and the raindrops his familiar step at the door. All about her conspired to torment.

From a place where bile seethes in twisted malice, the smell of her grief attracted a *Perelesnik*, the most deceitful of fiends, eager to feed on her pain. Concealed by darkness, it found its way to her home, filling its nostrils with her sorrow.

Closer, closer, it came, until it pressed insistently at her window, entering her dreams, where it took the sweet form of he who occupied her mind. The evil demon's true nature was more like scorched stubble or the rasp of a poisoned thorn catching tender skin.

Lightly, it tapped, and whispered soothing words of entreaty as she slept.

At last, she thought, *my darling has returned, as I've dreamt of these past nights.* Half-slumberous, she was drawn to the window.

'I've come for you my love,' murmured the wicked creature.

Entranced, she opened the shutter, and allowed it to stroke her cheek. Its touch was warm as she leaned her head against its palm. It would have taken but a moment for the demon to snap her slender neck.

'Come outside my sweet one, so that I might hold you,' it purred.

UNLATCHING THE DOOR, she stepped into the cool night.

Closer, closer, she walked, until it wrapped her in its arms and breathed its spell upon her, and she fell limply into its embrace.

It carried her with ease into the nearby shadows, where it lay her down. There, it lifted her gown, licking its lips at the thought of consuming not one soul but two.

Only one among us had the power to intervene.

Through the gloom, swooped the spirit of her true love, in the shape of a cuckoo, to peck the demon's eye. The beast swore all the evil oaths of the Damned and, in so doing, roused the girl from her trance.

The creature vanished, leaving her with a sense of having avoided some terrible danger. She returned to her bed, tortured by visions she could not explain.

Not long afterwards, the villagers gathered for

Dzyady, to honour those who had passed beyond life. Taking eggs and pancakes, and fine barley porridge with berries, they assembled in the graveyard at dusk, each visiting the place where their loved ones lay, leaving a portion of their picnic for the one lying below, and pouring a libation of their best *samogon*.

The young girl, belly-swollen, ripe and heavy, was left safe and warm at home, where she fell into a troubled sleep. The *Perelesnik* returned, snuffling at her window. She heaved herself up and, desirous only of beholding her lover, she followed the entreaties of that seductive voice.

Outside, the fiend beckoned her onwards. Each step was a trial, the baby kicking, as if in warning, but the enchantment of the demon drew her forward.

Closer, closer, she was pulled into danger, until she stood on the soft peat of the marshy bog.

We watched through newt eyes winking, as moonlight filtered weakly through the mist.

The demon enfolded her as if within a velvet cape and reposed her upon the turf. Its fetid breath smelt to her of wild orchids and its clammy touch was like the warmth of midsummer sun. Even the babe stopped its fluttering.

From damp holes and hiding places, we peeped from the eyes of dark crawlies, toads and turtles. We watched as she beckoned the creature to kiss her.

As the vile thing bent closer, a swallow appeared, sent from the other side of the veil, the spirit of the girl's true love possessing that dainty body. Intent on saving her from the foul fiend, it swooped and dived, chirping insistently. It flapped its wings, pecking in the face of evil, refusing to be swept aside, so decisive was its mission.

The creature batted at the bird repeatedly, but it was too swift to allow itself to be taken by a blow, so that the *Perelesnik* was obliged to rise and take chase.

So moved were we, the spirit horde, that we too played our part, such as we are able, summoning forth a mist to cloud the vision of that vile beast. Stumbling, its foot caught in a creeping weed and it tumbled, declaring devilish oaths.

The girl's reverie lifted and, rolling on her side, she saw her Beloved succumbing to the marsh's perilous mud. It shimmered around the flailing body, sucking down the unholy beast.

She reached to save her love, as she had done that fateful day at the lake. With the ooze soon to close over its head, the putrid creature roared in frustration, losing its power to shade her eyes. At last, she saw its true form: all claws and snarls.

Rejoicing, we lifted the fog, to witness the downfall of that loathsome beast.

Trembling, she realised how close she had stood to the edge of a precipice, thinking herself safe, when a terrible descent awaited her.

Her grief returned with full force and she wailed pitifully. So bruised was her heart, and her memories of her beloved so tainted, that she thought to let the shivering bog cover her, easing her departure from this land of nightmares.

As these dark thoughts called to her, the swallow returned, perching on her hand and cocking its head, seeking to comfort her.

In her belly, the baby stirred and stretched. Her weariness was suddenly so great that she had not the strength to move, or even shed a tear, but, as she looked at the little bird, it was as if a thread joined them, one breast to the other.

Lulled by its delicate song, she closed her eyes and slept on a mossy bed that night, guarded, unbeknownst to her, by souls who knew too well how close she had come to a death untimely.

With the morning light, she found her way home once more.

Thereafter, she dreamt not only of her beloved's kiss and of his gentle touch but of his laughter. Her sadness would come upon her unexpectedly: in the midst of milking the goats, or making her bed, or in stirring a pot of fragrant soup but, by day, each bird's melody contained his sweet merriment and, by night, her child's slumbering murmurs brought comfort, reminding her of her true love, who stood watch, even in death.

Such is our capacity to heal, love sending tendrils of hope and peace through the ruins of pain and loss.

Glossary

Dzyady: Belarus' Day of the Dead, when families pay their respects at the graves of relatives. The spirits of the departed are thought to revisit their loved ones in the form of birds, to comfort them in grief or to warn of danger.

Perelesnik: a fiend able to take any human form, with the intention of seducing its victim, then performing an act of violence.

71

AGAINST GREED AND INGRATITUDE

THERE WAS ONCE a young man not only feckless, but ungrateful. Ivan neither helped in the heavy work of the house, nor that of the farm. If he could find some excuse to slope away, he would do so. Hot pastries left cooling in the kitchen were never safe when he was about, finding their way into his fist as he slipped out the back door.

After a night carousing with his friends, he walked home past the graveyard. Being drunk, and lazy, the young wastrel took a shortcut through the old stones marking the burial places. So befuddled by drink was he that he took not the least precaution, failing even to touch the buttons of his jacket, which everyone knows is the surest way to protect yourself from evil wishes – of man and devil alike.

> We tell these stories because we must,
> We tell these stories, for now we know,
> The old ways have wisdom;
> Take heed: remember the old ways.

Uncouth churl that he was, on feeling the excesses of his ill-spent evening pushing down upon his bladder, he took out his pike and urinated against a headstone. A good, long, hot, yellow piss it was, and a great relief to be rid of it.

'There you are,' called he, to no one in particular, and thus to anyone listening. 'A small token of my esteem! A noble libation of finest *samogon* for you. Nevermind that I've enjoyed it first!'

With hardly any moon to cast light upon the deed, he might have thought that there were none to look upon him and witness his disrespectful attitude. Of course, we know better. Various eyes were upon him and, it must be said, not all with fair intent.

> How many lie uneasy in their grave?
> You're never alone, most of all in the dark.
> We watch from that other realm,
> and what foul fiends watch with us.
> So many whispers, if you care to listen.

Staggering through the gloom, he tripped over a bag of rags and fell into a bush of stinging nettles. He uttered curses crude enough to make Beelzebub blush. In fact, the bag of rags was none other than a creature, living and breathing, though he could hardly tell if it were man or woman.

We, spirits of the dark realm, seeing far more, could have told him it was neither, nor flesh of any kind.

'Out of my way, filthy thing!' young Ivan shouted, realising that the bundle of cloth had arms, legs and head.

'What's your business sitting here in a graveyard in the dead of night? I might have snapped my neck in two stumbling over your smelly self. Get yourself gone. No decent soul should be here at this time of night!'

The withered creature, whatever it was, cackled most merrily at this, being sorely amused. 'I see you've a sense of humour!' it rasped, spitting up a gob of slime upon the lad's boots. 'I like a good wit and you've more than most. Such men as you deserve all the help they require in making the world a jollier place, and I have just the thing.'

Ivan, with his arse itching all over, and being in no mood for small talk, was about to give the creature a kick for its trouble, and be on his way, when, from under its cloak, it pulled a little red hen.

'Take this,' uttered the thing inside the rags. 'Its eggs will be not only the tastiest you've had but will oblige the eater to tell nothing but the truth. Think what fun you can have with that!'

'Stupid crone...' muttered the cur, but he took the hen and made off home, without further mishap, and fell unconscious into his bed.

With eyeballs ready to burst from his skull, he woke to find the hen perched upon his chest, looking at him beadily. He would have wrung its neck on the spot, but that it had laid some eggs, all in a row, next to his pillow.

'Seven nice little eggs, all for me,' he thought, and pulled on his britches.

His two sisters were in the kitchen, kneading the bread as he entered. 'Up at last,' said one. 'Nice it is to lie in your bed 'til eight o'clock, as if there were no jobs to be done.'

'Really brother,' said the other. 'We work our fingers to the bone. Not that we mind, but we rarely hear a word of thanks!'

'Sisters dear,' said he. 'I know you love me, no matter your complaints, and for this, let me offer you each two of these fresh eggs. That leaves three for me, and I'll have them fried, with sour cream on the side, and a slice of bread. Don't skimp on the butter!'

The sisters tutted but set to work with the pan. Soon all three were sitting down to their meal, and most delicious those eggs were. Their chins dripped with yolks thick and creamy.

'You know sister,' said the older of the girls. 'You'd do better refraining from breakfast altogether, and lunch too. Your skirts are getting far too tight. If you get much fatter, the men won't be able to find where to poke you!'

No sooner had the words left her lips than the girl clapped her hand to her mouth. '*Whatever came over me?*' she thought.

'Not like yourself!' jeered the other. 'No one has trouble finding your hole. That's a bush watered by any man with a spare kopeck, as I know!'

She too then stoppered her mouth.

'What a wicked thing to say!' snapped the first, giving her sister's nose a bitter tweak, though it was no more than the truth. She was partial to a tumble, and all the more so if there were a few coins for her purse.

'This is all your fault,' said the second sister, turning to

Ivan. 'You come home reeking of drink and it puts us all in a bad mood!'

'We'd be better off if you fell down a hole and never came back,' said the other.

'That harpy last night must have been right!' thought Ivan. 'These eggs have uncommon powers.'

He returned to the hen, whose eyes were twinkling, and found twenty more eggs. What mayhem could he cause with such a generous nest? His quick wit and talent for tomfoolery soon showed him the way, and back he trotted to his sisters.

'Sisters dear,' said Ivan, offering the eggs to his beloved siblings, 'You're quite right. I'm a lazy good-for-nothing. Let me make amends. An old beggar gave me these. Make enough blini for the whole village and we can invite them round for a jig.'

The two continued to grumble, but did as he bade them, being eager to play hostess to the young men thereabouts.

The guests duly arrived to eat the pancakes, served with mushrooms and sour cream, and to dance. Of course, once everyone had eaten the eggs, they were obliged, no matter their disposition, to speak only the truth.

'Move your fat backside,' squawked the older sister, addressing the miller's daughter, of whom she was jealous. 'I've only agreed to this party so that I can enjoy a good stuffing later. No one wants to fondle a horse-face like you!'

'Shut your trap!' came the reply. 'Better still, shut all your orifices and save the men a bout of the itch.'

'Ladies, ladies,' interjected the pastor. 'No need to argue. You both have the elegance of a sow in her sty but it won't deter anyone from giving you a saucy ride. I'd oblige myself were it not that I've lost the ability to raise my maypole.'

The gathering soon descended into mayhem, as insults erupted in honest abandon. Amidst black eyes, pulled hair a-plenty and feet stomped-upon, the company departed in a terrible mood. Ivan considered the jape most entertaining.

Idle hands make the devil's work, as they say, and it was true that nothing delighted him more than shenanigans.

Eager to thank the old dame, and see if she might have something else for him, the jackanape waited until the moon was high and returned to the graveyard. This time, he saw her from afar, sitting upon a tomb, legs tucked under a body hunched and cloaked. Only her long nose protruded, and one scaly talon, holding a sharpened bone, with which she picked her teeth.

It looked quite as if she, or it, had been waiting for him.

'Foul you may be,' began Ivan, averting his nose from the stench of the creature's rags, 'But you understand me well. You first gift pleased me greatly. What else do you have to offer me? Give me another gift old crone, and I promise to use it well.'

'You see nothing and you know nothing,' hissed the wizened figure. 'It's time you looked beneath. Then you can decide what I understand.'

With that, the hag gobbled into her hand and threw the spittle into Ivan's face.

'Putrid wretch!' cried he, rubbing at his eyes. When he opened them once more, the creature had departed. Many hours seemed to have passed, as the sun was leering over the horizon, without its usual radiance. Rather, the world had taken on a gloomy hue. A veil of grey had fallen, thick with despair. At the edges of his vision, the shadows shifted in a strange manner, as if something moved within.

Much put out, Ivan set off home, feeling in need of some hot broth to warm his bones and lift his spirits.

He passed the forest, the dense leaves of which barely admitted light. Yet, he saw flickers of movement in that darkness, and heard sounds strange and disturbing, such as he had never noticed before. Concealed in the shadows were indistinct figures, their voices, seething and muttering.

Hurrying on, he came upon the woodcutter, known for his crotchety ways, wearing his usual red kerchief. However, in place of his round, bearded face, he had the head of a grizzled bear, and his hands were great paws, clutching axe and chains. Ivan stopped abruptly, unsure whether to flee.

'Good morning to you,' said the woodcutter, giving a civil nod of greeting.

Young Ivan could hardly reply, his voice having deserted him. And then he heard the woodcutter say, quite distinctly, 'Lazy cur! Mooching about. Never seen him do a day's work!'

'I b-b-beg your pardon. Is that you woodcutter?' stuttered Ivan, feeling put out at such forthright talk, even from a speaking bear.

'Of course it's me!' answered the woodcutter sharply. Ivan felt quite sure he heard that gruff voice add, 'And I've no time to stand chatting to the likes of you!'

As the bear turned away, a premonition came upon the lad: a vision of a tree, made unsteady by the wind, falling with a mighty crack and squashing the woodcutter beneath. Ivan made to call out a warning, but it was too late. The woodcutter bear was already out of sight.

Ivan walked on, towards the village, wrapping his jacket close around him. Here, more than ever, there seemed to be a damp and gloomy mist. His limbs grew heavy, and a sense of sadness oppressed him. He was unaccustomed to such melancholy, being always one for jest.

Next to cross his path was a man who preferred the company of his goats to any other. He scurried more than walked, rubbing at his mouse whiskers with little rodent paws. 'Out of my way,' his voice seemed to squeak, and then, out loud, a polite, 'Good day.'

'He'll live until he's 92, dying quietly in his bed, and won't be found for a week,' thought Ivan.

As he proceeded through that sinister fog, the lad met one person after another, each revealing themselves to be both man and beast, appearing as shrew or rat, goat, wolf or pig. Moreover, each emitted a distinctive smell, some of rotting cabbage, others of acrid manure, or the bitter-sweet fragrance of decaying lilies.

His eyes had opened to a disturbing vision of the world: of jealousy, cruelty, lechery and inconsolable loss.

Moreover, each person's fate was displayed to him: a girl most pure of heart would be poisoned by her envious twin; a nagging wife would be struck down cruelly by her husband, her place in their bed filled in haste by another; a lad would save his fiancé from drowning, but then die himself, leaving his love to drown in grief.

He saw, as we do, the villainous punished and innocent murdered, lives ending by foul means or unspeakable deeds. He saw greed, vanity, self-righteousness, violent intentions, hearts black-secreted and fingers ever-clutching. Some smelt of blood, and murder.

How we sighed, from our veiled kingdom, to see the burden of his eyes. No living soul, however irksome, should behold those hidden corners, where loathsome inclinations seethe and smoulder.

Knowledge lay heavy upon him, as if wicked gremlins sat upon his shoulders, their choking fingers at his neck, curled into his hair, whispering wretched foulness into his ears. He wondered how he had ever joked and laughed, surrounded as he was by vice and folly. Those odious, self-seeking manifestations were a cruel gift indeed: the whole world now repugnant.

'I wish I'd never clapped eyes on that filthy creature!' thought the lad. So filled was he with despair, he lost his former humour and thought to throw himself into the river and be done with it.

At last, at last, so moved were we by his sorry plight that we took him by the hand and led him to a brighter place, to the home of a maiden pure of thought. Fragrant as meadow flowers, her light shone through that shadow world, and her face was her own. Her skin glistened as if sprinkled with morning dew. He took her hand and the foul spell was broken. The dark shades lifted, and those about him returned to their former appearance. His radiant maiden, though quite plain of looks, had a brightness of eye most uncommon.

Looking at her, he saw soft harebells and joyous nodding daisies. Looking at him, she saw a face like a merry buttercup. They fell at once in love and Ivan lost no time in asking the girl to marry him. He resolved to mend his ways, no longer wasting his strength or wit on idle pursuits.

Aware only that the creature in the graveyard had led him to his true love, he resolved to return, to thank the crone, and to ask, again, if there was a gift to spare him.

How ungrateful is man!

Going once more to that place where death abides, and where the living have no seat, between the shifting mist, he sought long. The creature appeared not to wish itself found until Ivan, forgetting his noble resolutions, stamped his foot and let forth an oath of irritation.

Then, as if from thin air, the hag made herself known, her ragged form propped against an ancient gravestone.

I've been seeking you some good hour,' complained the lad. 'Don't you know that I'm to be wed? I've come to invite you to the festivities, and (he had the decency to blush just a little) if you have a gift for me, and for my bride, that would be delightful.'

The creature pursed its lips in annoyance. 'Trust this halfwit to find love where I intended to cast its eyes into the darker recesses, and for him to see purity where he should have beheld only deceit,' thought the foul thing. It had thought to use him as its instrument.

Determined yet to use his self-serving nature to its advantage, it croaked, 'I'll give you a gift,' reaching beneath the rags to remove a girdle. 'Place this beneath the threshold of the cottage in which the wedding festivities are held, to bring new life to every guest. You'll see at last all my intentions for your future happiness.'

She raised her head to reveal a face narrow and whiskery, eyes lizard yellow, filled with malign cunning. Fool that he was, Ivan took the girdle, and did just as she suggested, imagining some light-hearted caper or escapade would ensue, to bring jollity to the celebrations. Any man with more sense would have kept well away.

A great band of well-wishers attended the ceremony, with no woman looking more beautiful than Ivan's gentle new bride. Afterwards, the merry company returned to his home for the marriage feast.

However, as each foot stepped across the threshold, it was transformed. Dainty feet in felt slippers and big feet in wooden clogs, children's feet in cloth boots and old women's gnarled toes: all grew sharp-nailed and hairy. And, mid-sentence, their heads flung back, to emit a howl. Each hand turned to a paw and teeth became long fangs. Filled with brutal thirst, they gnashed at one another's throats, ripping flesh asunder.

Come morning, only the groom remained, demented with grief, his bride's bloodied kerchief in his hand. When evil forces walk, the innocent too should tremble.

Beware accepting gifts from strangers.

Beware trusting those you know not.
Beware your greed.
Beware mischief-making.
And beware, beware, beware all things
which creep in the shadows.
You're not alone.
Never alone
Here, in the dark.

AGAINST LECHERY

The banya – or bath-house – is not only a place for washing. It holds its own vital powers, as a place of birthing and for ritualistic cleansing, such as on the night before a wedding. The spirit of the banya is the Bannik. A demon long of limb and beard, with temperament mischievous and variable, it is unwise to upset him. Moreover, after three firings of the stove, the banya becomes the domain of the Bannik and his demon guests from the forest, making a further visit ill-advised. To look into his eyes is to be struck immobile with fear.

At New Year, the banya demon may be consulted on whether the coming months will bring happiness or disappointment by offering your back to him through the half-open door. A spiteful clawing or soft caress can indicate the nature of what lies ahead.

The turning of the old year to the new is a time of magic, especially of foretelling what is to come. Our tale unfolds on one such night, as wolves prowl with jaws ice-locked and the moon hangs bare.

> Hear our stories, learn from our errors.
> We too, were once flesh and blood.
> Take heed: remember the old ways.

In a small village, much like any other, a family party assembled to welcome the New Year. The mother of the house had prepared rich dishes, diverse and delicious, ensuring that the table was well laden. Their manner of gathering on this night would determine the abundance of their table for the times to come.

The dust had been swept clean from the corners and brushed out the door, taking with it all hint of misfortune, and one little window was ajar, to allow the freshness and joy of the New Year to enter.

Reminded not to utter any foul oaths, or to argue, or shed tears, since this could only bring future days of conflict and unhappiness, the party feasted and the merriment of the table finally turned to fortune-telling.

There were five young daughters of the household, eager to know the identity of their future husbands. Being that night inclined to entertain the girls in their childish fancies, their mother placed several rings in a dish of grain.

With eyes closed tight, each placed her hand within the bowl, being encouraged to withdraw a small portion and see what lay within. The youngest, not yet thirteen, held only grain: her life would not change in the coming months. The next, three years older, withdrew the ring of her secret delight, one belonging to her grandmother; with a cry of satisfaction, she proclaimed her wish not to marry yet at all, but to have a new dress and bonnet in time for spring.

Her older sisters rolled their eyes and examined their own palms. Despite being of marriageable age, they were all three without offers. They each boasted a fine figure and reasonable looks, but were dour, vain and jealous in turn, which had deterred their suitors.

The first sister, Masha, held a ring of copper. Irinka, the oldest, held a silver ring, and the third, Olga, held gold.

Masha sighed dolefully, since the copper ring denoted that she would marry a poor man. She threw it back into the bowl, declaring the game nonsense.

Irinka, clutching her silver ring, smiled smugly; hers indicated a man of modest means but with a good heart. Her long wait for marriage must surely be over.

Olga held her golden ring aloft triumphantly. The meaning was plain: a wealthy marriage awaited her. She tossed her head, already imagining herself in rich gowns, the envy of her sisters.

So it was that, as midnight approached and the family continued their revelry, the three older girls excused themselves, professing their wish to consult the *Bannik* about the accuracy of these predictions. The mischievous spirit of the *banya* is not usually one to be meddled with;

however, on New Year's Eve, he is known for his willingness to be approached.

Outside in the shadows was the innkeeper, stamping his felt-booted feet against the cold and wriggling his numb fingers. Few in the village had a good word for him. His wife, now departed, had been a downtrodden wretch, rarely shown kindness. Their only son had long since left to make his own way in the world. Grizzled and lecherous, the old man now had his eye on the daughters of the house. His bed had been cold too long and the thought of supple flesh filled his dreams. His beady eyes had been watching the jovial scene, through the window.

The innkeeper, having overheard the girls' intention, was struck with desire to see them naked. He scuttled into the *banya*, having concealed his clothes inside his coat, and placed them under nearby bushes.

On entering, he splashed a generous ladle of water on the coals, so that the room filled with dense steam, hiding him from view, in the far corner.

The girls, close behind, were surprised to find the *banya* already filled with vapour but were too intent on their purpose to pay much heed. They set about washing, knowing that the *Bannik* liked everyone to be clean before asking him to tell their fortune.

Having taken a few jugs of beer, the girls felt rather giddy, and teased each other with more than a hint of rivalry. The oldest of the three, vain Irinka, declared herself the most favoured, having the largest bosom. This she jiggled provocatively and defied the others to deny it.

The mist was clearing a little, and the innkeeper received a tantalising glimpse. Licking his lips, he cast another ladle of water, so that the room became thick once more. He had a plan.

Moving stealthily, he reached out his hands, feeling hopefully for the curve of those glorious breasts and, finding them, gave a squeeze.

'You cheeky things,' laughed the girl, imagining that her own siblings were the culprits. 'Well? Don't you agree? Aren't they the finest?'

The innkeeper gave each rosebud a tweak, making the girl squeak and slap his hands away.

'What a jealous pair you are!' Irinka cried.

Olga scoffed, although she secretly envied her sister's ample bosom. 'A fine opinion you have of yourself. Don't forget that men like curves behind as well as up front.'

Saying this, she bent over and slapped her buttocks. Her sisters could not help but giggle at her playful vulgarity and each gave her a slap in turn. As the vapours lifted a little, the innkeeper, crouched once more in his corner, enjoyed an advantageous view.

The vile voyeur placed a third cup of water on the coals, so that the three young women could barely see their own hands before them. The innkeeper moved silently through the steam, until his round, hairy stomach found Masha, sitting on a lower bench.

'Somebody's eaten too much pastry tonight,' taunted the girl, patting the innkeeper's belly. 'You won't catch a husband with a fat tummy!'

Her sisters, oblivious to the presence of a fourth among them, could not but agree. 'True enough, sister,' they murmured, thinking she spoke of herself.

The innkeeper pushed forward, so that his swollen and sweaty stump nudged the poor girl on the chin.

'Oi! Keep your elbows to yourself!' she squealed, jerking her own upwards, and catching her target with full force.

Caught unawares, he had a little of the beast knocked out of him, and slunk back, nursing his treasures.

At last, the three decided that the time had come to ask the *Bannik*'s advice. He must surely be close by, being responsible for the abundant steam.

The sisters departed to wait in the annex, each taking her turn to tentatively offer her back, through the half-open door, bracing for the *Bannik*'s prophetic gesture.

Would he grant them a caress or a clawing? The innkeeper crept forward, reaching towards the first unsuspecting girl. He stroked her back, then gave her meaty rump a greedy pinch. Masha let out a shriek but refused to admit what had happened, telling her sisters that she'd stubbed her toe on the door. The *Bannik*, she said, had given her a good omen.

The second stepped into the doorway, the steam wafting about her. She waited anxiously, yet eagerly. Two hands reached for her, stroking her back tenderly, from the very top, down to the cleft of her rounded cheeks. Then, Olga heard a low chuckle and felt her buttocks clasped firmly. She stood all a-tremble, enduring the unexpected fondle.

Not a word did she utter, despite her surprise and consternation. She merely nodded to her sisters on return, indicating that she too had received a favourable omen. She had no intention of giving them the satisfaction of scorning her.

By now, Irinka could hardly contain her excitement, feeling certain that the *Bannik* would caress her as he had done her sisters. If anyone would have the fortune of gaining a husband in the coming year, it would be her, she thought, being most deserving of admiration! Re-entering the vapours, and picturing the promise of the gold ring in her mind's eye, she offered her back to the presence within, awaiting its touch.

The randy innkeeper had enjoyed far too much excitement for one night and could control himself no longer. Seeing the last girl's back, he grasped her about the hips and thrust himself at her ample behind, rubbing lewdly against her soft skin. Hardly anticipating such an assault, she gasped in shock and jumped out of the clinch, back to the safety of the outer room. As to whether the embrace was one of ill-omen or good, on reflection, she decided that it must be a sign of extreme favour and decided it best to accept her good luck.

The sisters dressed hurriedly, heading back through the night to home and bed, then they took to their pillows, each dreaming of a wedding and the excitement of the marriage bed. It must be said, they recalled their recent caresses with more pleasure than they could decently admit.

The wicked innkeeper stayed within the *banya*, waiting until his path of escape might be clear. The evening had been a great success. The sampling of warm, young flesh had been worth every moment he'd spent lingering in the cold.

Such rascally behaviour cannot go unpunished. It is such churls who come to join our ranks, in the unquiet hereafter. The lecherous old reprobate was about to leave when he heard a deep growl behind him. He hardly dared look, but saw eyes glowing through the vapours - not one pair but several, eyes glowing red, and yellow, and sickly green, those of the Bannik and his demon guests. In a trice, a hairy paw seized him.

The *Bannik*'s long, wiry beard tickled the old man's ear but there was nothing playful in the demon's grip about his neck. It was determined to wreak its revenge on the old man for daring to impersonate him, particularly with such lewd motives!

The creatures chased the inn-keeper about the room, delivering terrible slaps to his bony backside, each one harder than the last, so that the miscreant's posterior was scorched tender.

With a snarl, the *Bannik* dug its claws into the man's flesh, peeling back the wrinkled skin. How the rogue did howl! At last, tiring of his cries and growing hungry, the fiendish gathering grasped legs and arms, pulling until the innkeeper's limbs were rent asunder. These, they tossed onto the hot coals, so that the flesh sizzled and the smell of scorched human meat filled their nostrils. The demons devoured him, every piece, snapping his bones, and licking blood and melting fat from their chins.

> Easy fruits for evil appetites,
> our flesh, a tasty afterthought,
> our bones flung asunder.

Sucking the last morsel from its talons, the *Bannik* congratulated itself on saving the delightful ladies of the household from wedlock to a groom so undeserving.

Hear our stories, take heed.
We watch, but the demons watch too.

AGAINST TRICKERY IN LOVE

THERE WAS ONCE a girl so entirely wily that nothing she desired had ever been denied her. The art of manipulation came as naturally as the gift of song comes to the lark.

Plotting and scheming were her art: to gain more attention, more flattery, more pretty things, yet her face betrayed none of this. In truth, she was a beauty, which conspired to make others easy prey to her wiles.

By the time she had reached womanhood, every man danced to her tune, and she was at liberty to choose as she pleased.

Of course, we always desire what remains out of reach and so it was that her determination set upon the black-smith's son. Broad-shouldered and strong, he was hand-some enough for any girl with her sights set high.

To her chagrin, pursue him as she might, he rebuffed her. He, wiser than most, had no time for her charms, which he viewed as precocious.

Infatuated as she was, she resolved to creep by night

through his window, and slip into his bed, seeking to sway his flesh, if nothing else.

We watched, unblinking, from the dark corners, witnesses to her deceitful seduction.

As he slumbered, her gentle strokes raised his ardour; she had little difficulty in provoking his engorged desire.

'Ha!' thought she. 'You're just a man! Mine to command in sleeping lust.'

Gleefully, she took his slippery cock between her thighs, and rocked upon its length.

How wicked it is to trick a man, to take advantage of his natural reactions to a knowing caress. For even while a man's mind is sleeping, his flesh, with a cunning touch, may be persuaded to have thoughts of its own.

We spirits, too, are obliged against our will: to watch the sins and perversions of the world forever more, in atonement for our earthly misdeeds.

Before the lad could fill her with his seed, we sent a little mouse beneath the covers, to nibble at his toes.

Roused, he perceived the wench's guile.

'Damnable Eve! Out with you!' he cried, and bundled her through the window, to land in the mud.

Most would have hung their head in shame, or turned in vengeance upon the source of their unrequited love but not she.

'He'll yet be mine!' she vowed.

When such a mind is set, nothing can turn it from its path.

She visited a crone who lived in the forest, all alone: an ancient hag, known for her healing, and wisdom, and other skills hardly daring of mention.

'I need the old ways,' beseeched the girl. 'I need a spell to cast upon the blacksmith's son, to make him mine. I'll possess him yet, even if the devil take my soul for it!'

How easily the young do utter such words, without a thought for the consequences. To hear them sent a shiver even to our bleak realm, and stirred lurking malice from its slumber. Talons that would clutch at human folly unfurled, in readiness.

The old woman shuddered at the wench's rashness.

'If you take the path of old magic I set you upon, there'll be no turning back,' she warned, a prickle rising even then on the back of her wrinkled neck.

But, having suffered indignity, the girl would not be counseled to turn from her path, however imprudent. She'd conquer the blacksmith's son at any cost.

'Help me, or I'll take a tinder from your hearth and set this cottage ablaze,' declared the girl.

And so, in answer to this threat, the crone gave her all she asked for, and gladly, knowing that the ill-mannered slut, so coddled and cossetted, would soon regret her petulance.

'Do this, and you shall receive what you desire, and sevenfold,' promised the hag. If the girl had thought to look, she'd have seen malicious intent in the old woman's eye, clouded though it was.

The crone made all clear. The girl was to write the name of her love upon four pieces of paper, each anointed with the scent of her desire. She stole a letter from her father's chest, and tore it into pieces, pressing each against her eager cunt, soaking them with her anticipation, with her hunger.

The first, she was to place inside the hole of an ancient oak in the forest, reputed for its magic. She crept there in the indigo hours, when men sleep and wild places awaken. The night callings of creatures winged and tailed and clawed accompanied her steps, and echoed the beating of her covetous heart.

The second was to be buried deep in the soil, at a crossroads. As she pushed the paper beneath, the moist earth dirtied her nails and hands, begrimed evidence of her obsession.

The third, she was to wrap about a stone and throw into a fast-flowing river. The magical rune sank deep and deeper, past fish-eyes and eels, and the blink of newts. It found a resting place in the murky mud and no creature came near.

The fourth was to be burnt, unseen by human eye. Though no man or woman was there to observe her, other eyes were watching. Eyes unearthly and inhuman.

With the last, the girl would summon help from places dark, to which no words should be offered, and no promises made.

She performed each task as the wise old woman had directed. Nigh the witching hour, she sat before her fire, alone, all others safely abed.

It was then that she uttered her song of enchantment, as the witch had taught her: a song to summon the demonic dark.

And the room grew chill.

Her words were thus, to stir obsession in the heart of the blacksmith's son, and place him entirely in her power. She called upon Chernobog and all the darkling sky to hear her. She called on the teeth of the dead, and the breath of the living:

> May longing gnaw his bones,
> Blossom in his veins.
> May he ache with lust,
> Wracked with keen-edged pain.
> May he thirst forever,
> May he never quench desire,
> Knowing neither rest nor ease,
> Until he my bed acquire.

As the spell left her lips, the shadows stretched taller, reaching to clutch at the very breath upon which the incantation was carried.

The spirit guardians of the home have no sway when the hateful shadows of the underworld are invited within, and nor do we, the silent watchers. So much we've seen. So much we cannot forget. We sent the flickering flames of the hearth to burn brighter, to consume the fiends, but to no avail.

Forces tantalizing and treacherous, of guile, seduction, duplicity and deceit seeped under the mantel of the door. They oozed from the corners the room, and crept under the thatch. Forces fiendish befouled the wholesome hearth, dark enchantment smothering those bright guardian flames. When she retired, they slithered under the sheets to share her bed.

She slept fitfully, in dreams half-lustful, half-terrified, in which her lover's hands, welcome upon her body, transformed into talons, and the sweet breath of desire turned putrid. Suspended in a place fathoms dark, strange hands emerged from the abyss to clutch at her, nails sharp scraping her flesh.

Awake as the first light entered the world, she rose and left the house, eager to greet her love. She passed by his window, to whisper his name, believing that he would hear, and follow.

She walked to the river, where lovers often swam and fondled, the waters concealing their ardour, and undressed, leaving her clothing on the bank. She slipped the cool mantle of the water upon her naked skin, and waited, limbs moving pale and sinuous under the water, feeling certain that he would come.

All was silent, not a creature stirring. Neither cry of bird, nor the occasional lazy flip of fish in the water was apparent to the girl.

And then, she saw him. Her heart leapt with triumph at the sight: he, with dark locks long and tousled, and eyes only for her. She watched exultant as he removed his jacket, his shirt, his trousers. He stood upon the bank, cock thick and bobbing.

'Come in, my love,' she cried to him. 'I've waited long for you to claim me.'

But he made no move.

She saw another stride forward to stand at his side. Another just the same: another blacksmith's son, identical in every way. He too removed his clothes and, as he did so, a third man joined the pair: all three the same in looks and stature.

She did not utter a word, as fear grew now within her.

How could there be three of he she knew to be just one?

A fourth appeared, and yet more, until seven blacksmith's sons waited on the bank to greet her, each naked, and with all the desire evident that she had so longed for.

'Speak to me!' she cried at last. 'Who are you? If some demon vision from the underworld, come to taunt me, I wish you be gone!'

The seven ignored her plea, offering neither smile nor frown. Faces implacable they cast upon her, as if she had no more value to them than a frog in the mud.

And yet, they beckoned to her, inviting her to leave the water and join them on the bank.

'I won't come to you,' she vowed. 'This is trickery! Unfair deceit! Return to whence you came, whatever demons you be, and send my true love here.'

But they did not.

The seven stepped forward, each taking a path through the reeds, to enter the cool water's edge.

Closer, closer, closer.

She wondered to where she might flee, but the seven were soon almost upon her, first covered to their knee, and then their hip, until they were swimming out to her, each with a face unfeeling.

Closer, closer, closer.

Perhaps, she thought, one is my true love, and will reveal himself. She turned from one to the other, looking at each, seeking he she knew so well.

Closer, closer, closer.

But each man's eyes were dead to her; dark and expressionless, conjured as they were from that place unholy, conjured by the ill-intent of her spell, conjured to serve her justly, with sevenfold repayment. Encircling the girl, the seven grasped her in firm embraces, shoving her one to the next, fingers plucking at her fear-chilled flesh, stabbing at yielding softness.

'Where is my love?' she thought. 'Perhaps he's here, and this is a test, to which I must submit. Perhaps I must recognise him amongst this throng.'

Rough and rougher, one to the next, they pushed her. Cold hands squeezed with bruising malice. They pierced and stabbed her, their eyes ever vacant. There can be no mercy from creatures unearthly. She surrendered her body and hatefully they took her, and tore her and broke her: sevenfold punishment for wicked intentions.

The water closed over her head, at last, at last. Gasping, she sank down, down to the darkest of dark. Creatures rose from the depths to claim her, to drag her down, from where she was never seen again.

So it is that human folly is served. Take heed. Dark forces are best left where they lurk, in the shadow-realm. We whisper our warning, here in our darkness. Wishes and deeds steeped in deceitful intent will have deceitful ends.

GLOSSARY

Chernobog: the dark, accursed deity, thought to summon demons to his bidding

AGAINST CAUTION

Kupalle night has been celebrated, since pagan times, in June, 'the beautiful month'. Coinciding with the summer solstice, it is a time of magic, of forecasting the future, and of revelling in the power of nature, water and fire. Under cover of darkness, all manner of lusty behaviour is indulged. Amidst this gaiety, it is also a time for evil creatures to roam, intent on havoc. Animals are kept safely in their barns, with talismans hanging to protect them. People who wander in meadow and forest are wise to keep their wits about them.

THERE WERE ONCE TWO SISTERS, plump and plain, and with little wit or talent. They came from a humble home of modest income. As they became young women, they had little to recommend them. Meanwhile, their father, a vinegary, bearish old widower, was in no haste to let them depart, wishing them to keep house, bake and scrub. To the girls' dismay, he offered no dowry and made no overtures to possible suitors.

Each year, on *Kupalle*'s Eve, raising their hopes, the

two would join in making garlands for their hair, gathering buttercups, and fragrant chamomiles, cornflowers of deep blue, ribwort and thistles, delicate violets and briar rose blooms, daisies and dandelions. These garlands they threw into the river, standing alongside the other village girls, sending the wreaths downstream, for the young men to chase. However, no young man ever attempted to fish out the garlands of the two hopeful sisters, leaving them to drift aimlessly with the current, to spin and to sink.

The girls would join in singing flirtatious songs, and in raising their skirts high as they jumped over the flames of the *Kupalle* bonfire. They would dance with abandon, and lick their fingers suggestively as they consumed the *kulaha* pudding and sweet *vereniki*, casting teasing looks at the men about them. However, their efforts were all in vain.

Before laying their heads down to sleep, they would place the leaves of twelve different plants beneath the pillows of their shared bed, wishing to dream of the husbands who would one day join them between the sheets.

Into the linens, one sister would whisper:

> You who live by the road,
> You see young and old,
> Tell me of my betrothed!

While the other, stroking the soft flesh of her inner thigh would intone:

My-one-true-betrothed,
Come to my garden to stroll!

Alas, all was to no avail, and the sisters lamented that they would die unloved, unwedded and childless. The years passed and the girls despaired, believing they were fated to remain old maids in their father's house.

THE DARK HOURS of *Kupalle's* Eve are also known as the Night of Love, when the usual rules of propriety are set aside. The young, hot with desire, enter the forest, under pretext of seeking the magical *Chervona Ruta,* a flower said to bring all good fortune.

On such nights, desire is ignited and virginity lost, babes are conceived, and couples betrothed. Here are riches indeed, and pleasure guaranteed.

Perhaps a little mouse whispered in their ear, or it may have been the sigh of the wind, or the gentle caress of our midnight voices, for we are wont to make suggestions as you sleep, but, at last, the two sisters were of one mind, and made a pact to change their destiny.

They decided, at last, to throw caution to the wind and, on this night of *Kupalle*, enter the forest, in search of what they could no longer live without.

First, they watched each courting pair, hands grasped, scamper beneath the branches. Then came those not yet promised, those beckoning, those unattached; girls, and then men, off into the shadows.

The sisters took their own path, eyes wide open and

seeking, seeking. And we, entwined on the cool breeze of the night air, followed.

The night was beetle-dark. With thick foliage and little moonlight to help them, the way was confusing. Branches reached to trip them, and spiteful thorns and nettles pinched their arms. They began to wonder what had possessed them. Little mushrooms, centipedes and lizards, night-kissing bats and their moth-lovers; all creatures furry, scaly and winged, all cocked their heads as the two passed by, yet, though the sisters strained their ears, there was only stillness: not even a far off squeal to lend encouragement.

The forest, watching, held its breath, and we trod the path behind.

At last, the girls came upon a place, in that gloom, which they recognised: a glade in which was located a very old and half-rotten oak, with a hole through its middle. Old, old it was, and known as a conspirator in magic spells. It was said that good luck would befall any who slithered through the opening of the ancient tree.

'Let's rest here awhile,' suggested the elder of the two. 'If we sit quietly, and listen, we may hear someone approach.'

'What fortune to have stumbled on this place,' remarked the younger. 'We should pass through the oak, as we did when we were little, for good luck. On this night of such magic, it may further avail us.'

She poked her head through, then arms; she wriggled and wriggled, but found she was stuck. Her dimensions had grown since she'd last attempted the feat. The other gave a push, and then another, but served only to jam her poor sibling further inside.

'I have a plan,' said the elder and, moving round to the opposite side of the tree, reached deep into the hole, past her sister's head and arms, until she was nearly forehead to forehead with her, and clutched either side of her sibling's skirts. These she pulled, hoping to drag her through and out the other side, but without success.

Can you guess?

Now, the elder was stuck, legs waving as she tried to extract herself. If only their brains had been as well-endowed as their bottoms.

'What shall we do?' asked the younger.

'Someone is sure to find us,' replied the other. 'Close your eyes and wish very hard. Wish for someone with strong arms to find us.'

'Someone with strong arms and broad shoulders,' said the first.

'Someone with strong arms, broad shoulders and large hands,' said the other.

'Someone with strong arms, and broad shoulders, and large hands, and…determination,' the younger ventured.

So they waited.

Time passed, although they could not have said whether it were two minutes or twenty.

At last, they heard a footstep, and then another – slow and heavy. Someone had arrived and was walking about the tree in all deliberation, surveying the sight… and what a sight it was!

When the voice spoke, it was not any they recognised, and its timbre was deep and manly, such as to raise a shiver on their skin: it was a voice of promise and menace.

'Few have ever wished for me quite so ardently,' it told the sisters, its words sending the oak vibrating with strange resonance. 'You called and I am here. I will help, but I must have my price. Payment is always required, and I believe I know what is in your hearts. It will suffice.'

'Yes, yes,' the women squeaked from their confine within the tree. 'We'll do anything you require, but please pull us free.'

At that, the demon – for such it was, and no man at all – lifted the skirts of the elder sister.

We'd followed them to the forest, a-nipping at their heels, nudging them forward in search of muscle and meat, such as every young girl deserves, but here was more than they had bargained for.

Still, we stayed close.

The fiend yanked at her bloomers, to expose her lavish bottom: how ripe, how lush, how delectable that flesh. Its hands were large, hot, and hairy. Its shoulders were broad, its arms strong, and determined it was. Very determined indeed. It gave her a slap, at which she squealed. Then it gave her much more, at which she gasped. The deed did not take long.

The creature then went to settle its account on the other side of the tree. Here was a rump jiggling in readiness. The younger sister, despite the discomfort of her situation, could not deny her delight. How she had dreamed of this rough seduction, and who can deny the thrill of an illicit coupling…

Once it had enjoyed its fill, the demon mused. Usually,

it would have guzzled them up, in a few quick bites. Plenty of nourishment on these bones, and juices to help the meal slide down. However, the fiend was weary of its usual habits. Malevolence is an easy pastime. It fancied a change.

Such are the whims of dark creatures, and creeping things, which have not the consistency of conscience to govern them. Luckily for the two wenches, the ghoul chose to extend the reach of its amusement.

It stretched the hole in the oak, and the two women tumbled to the ground, damson-faced and breathless. The tree, also, was much relieved.

'Now,' pronounced the fiend. 'Are you feeling brave?'

The pair were not. In fact, now that they could see the demon in all its horrible glory — hairy and gnarled in the strangest of places — they were all a-tremble. However, they felt that it would be sensible to nod.

'Delightful!' it said, giving a smile intended more to unnerve than encourage. So, it led them, hands held, grasped firmly by those uncommonly large demon-hands. And we walked behind.

As they went deeper into the forest, the sisters either side of the ghoul, they saw more than they had before. Where the darkness had been silent, the trees were now filled with chatter, every woodlouse, shrew and squirrel remarking on their parade.

'Look at that,' cooed a pigeon. 'There's trouble.' It hid its head under its wing.

'Stomping through, with no care for who they're treading on,' grumbled a worm, just below the leaves. 'And in bad company too. Flesh soon to return to the earth;

worms in and worms out. There's always work for us to do.'

Further on, they came across a courting couple, grunting in the bushes. They paused to watch, just for a moment.

'Look all you like,' leered the demon. 'While I have hold of you, they won't see you at all.' It appeared quite true.

'Close your eyes now,' the fiend commanded, and it led them such a twisting path that they could never have said how they arrived. When it permitted them again to look, before them, they saw a sight such as might have dropped them dead there and then, had they not been young and robust.

All that is most horrifying to man, and much else besides, was gathered: a host of creatures foul and putrid, enjoying a party of most peculiar and noisy invention.

There was twirling and toasting, gobbling and choking, leaping and chattering, clappering and clawing. Noses were tweaked and feet rough-stamped, elbows poked and hair harsh-twitched, ears boxed and nails steely-scraped.

Rat-faced and crow-clawed, lips stained blood-crimson with gorged forest bounty, they grinned in welcome. Seeds, fur and feathers stuck in their teeth, suggesting a feast of sloes and blackberries-dark, and the flesh of scamper-bys, birds and bats.

'You've brought the next course then,' called one of the loathsome band.

'Such dainty fruit,' smirked another, 'Full-blown and heavy and ready to burst. It will only take a little squeeze.'

'Come and give mine a squeeze little girlies,' cackled the next, thrusting suggestively. 'Suck 'em till your lips are numb.'

'Slurp them,' leered one, tongue lashing suggestively.

'Chomp them,' squawked another.

Creeping, slithering, the creatures crawled closer, striking dread in the poor sisters where they stood. Hideous forms looming out of the dark, they scratched and scrabbled, jostling to be foremost.

'Grind them,' gibbered one grisly and gruff.

'Carve them,' crowed another. Drool hung from its chops.

Each malicious proposition was more appalling than the last, a cacophony of savage smut and maniacal gestures.

'Pound them.'

'Poke them.'

'Slice them.'

'Splice them.'

The girls clutched hands in terror, but kept their eyes open, as suggestions seethed, one upon the other.

The chief demon surveyed with amusement, its claws firmly upon the shoulders of the wenches, and foetid breath hot upon their necks. It licked its lips.

'Crush them,' squawked one of cankerous crowd.

Trembling, the sisters pressed together, back-to-back, fingers entwined, eyes seeking escape.

'Shred them.'

'Split them.'

The filthy gang encircled.

'Bite them.'

'Skin them.'

Through a small gap between hooves and talon-sprouted feet, the older sister spied something glowing, glowing red like the warm hearth fire of home. Beyond this stinking gaggle, came into sight the delicate fronds of the *Chervona Ruta*, the fabled fern, red as wrath.

'Gouge them,' gloated one of the creatures, its grasping claws but a hair's breadth away.

Voices shrill and howling engulfed the two.

'Pulp them.'

The younger wench began to scream.

'Peel them.'

'Courage, dear sister,' shouted the elder, eyes upon the magical fern.

'EAT THEM!'

'No! No!' shrieked the pair.

At that, despite its pleasure in this mirthful scene, the demon declared, 'Stay fast night-crawlers. Before you have your fun, we must give these women of wit and beauty their chance to win the treasure of *Kupalle*'s Eve: the bloom which flowers but once a year, in these dark hours.'

Such mockery there was: hoots of derision, heckling and jeering, tattle-taunting and tongue-wagging, scoffing and scorning.

The two wenches were as good as gobbled.

'Quick about it then!' screeched one among the odious bunch.

The rank assembly fell back, hushed, to reveal the tiny flower where it grew, bathed in scarlet radiance.

Granted its voice, the bloom began to speak, casting its question to the trembling women.

> 'Here is my riddle, wenches two,
> What begins well,
> But may rust?
> As you know to be true.
>
> What bruises and bleeds,
> As time passes by?
> Upon what do men feed,
> Though women may sigh?
> What is juiciest in Spring,
> But, by Winter, may dry?
>
> What promises the world,
> But may rot and decay?
> Corrupted by false words,
> Your heart it will slay?'

The sisters looked about at the diabolical company, each face etched with hate and malice, with disgruntlement and grievance, as if every vexation known to man were there engraved and brought to life in vengeful purpose.

How many souls had these creatures devoured, nourished by man's envy, and lust and vanity?

They knew what they had sought, like so many other girls, and what lay out of reach, though so ardently yearned for.

The answer was 'love'.

As soon as the word was uttered, the detestable society cried out in fearsome rage, knowing their vile intentions to have been thwarted, although the chief demon smiled to itself at their escape, knowing that his reach would have its time another day.

The sisters ran forward to pluck the bloom and, upon touching its enchanted petals, found themselves once more alone, in the still and silent gloom, but this time, with the forest edge in sight, all peril melted into the first rays of coming dawn.

THE FERN, in its magic, brought them the gift of detecting all things hidden: from the true thoughts of men to the very secrets concealed beneath the earth. They gained some glimpse of what we see, from the edges, concealed from the realm of humankind.

Thus it was that they became rich not only in wisdom but in material wealth, the flower leading them to the hidden places in which treasure had been buried long ago and long forgotten.

Seeing into the hearts of others, they gained knowledge of how to please and, being of independent means, received suitors aplenty.

However, the sisters were now in no rush to marry. They moved from their father's home and bought a farm of their own, upon which they employed only the strongest of men, to perform the rough work.

They lived very happily ever after.

. . .

So it is that demons do not always have their way, and poor humans may outwit their evil clutches. We spirits know that caution is the surest path but, without venture, what can there ever be gained? Sometimes, the heart must be brave, and we must strike out for what we desire.

Glossary

Kulaha: a pudding made of wheat

Vareniki: dumplings stuffed with berries

Chervona Ruta or fern flower: on Kupalle night, it is said that the magical fern's fronds will turn from yellow to red. In the face of demons, which would lead you astray, you must remain resolute and grasp the flower, having passed a certain test. Power to see beneath the soil will then be yours, enabling you to discover treasure.

AFTERWORD

Look into the flames of our fire.
    Gaze upon the smouldering embers.
    We're whispering there.
    We know the shade and umber of your soul,
    Of all you covet,
    We know what lies beneath.

    You've heard our tales,
    of lust and rivalry,
    Greed and envy,
    of concealments and secrets,
    Tales of demons,
    intent on mischief and retribution.

    Did you listen
    Listen with your eyes and your lips,
    Your skin and your blood?
    Did you hear us,
    from the edges

whispering to you, warning you?
Did you feel the touch
of talons on your skin?
When you close your eyes,
did creatures malevolent gaze back at you?
Is your shadow on the wall
really yours, after all?

You may pull the covers tighter to your chin
but remember,
They'll creep in beside you.
We all have our dark bedfellows.

We tell these stories because we must,
We tell these stories, for now we know.
Remember the old ways, in all their wisdom.

Taste the ice-hot pleasure of desire.
  Tend to the hearth of your loved one's fire,
  laugh, cry, embrace and sigh.
  Savour the deep warmth of sun, the sweet chill of winter
frost,
  the glint of streams, the gleam of moon's light
  Drink deeply. Drink deeply.

You do not know how long your feet may walk the earth,
  As we knew not what awaited after death.

Only the stars know.
  Only the seas,
  Only the wind.

As we watch, are watching, ever watching,
from beyond, and behind and below

Hear our stories, learn from our errors,
take heed.
Cleave to your courage.
Value your light.

For they are watching you.

GLOSSARY

Banya: an outside bath-house, used as a sauna, with an ante-room often used for disrobing. Not only a place for washing, it is thought to have its own powers, being once used as a place of birthing and for ritualistic cleansing, such as on the night before a wedding.

Bannik: The spirit of the banya. A demon long of limb and beard, with temperament mischievous and variable, it is unwise to upset him. After three firings of the stove, the banya becomes the domain of the Bannik and his demon guests from the forest, making a further visit ill-advised. To look into his eyes is to be struck immobile with fear. At New Year, the banya demon may be consulted on whether the coming months will bring happiness or disappointment by offering your back to him through the half-open door. A spiteful clawing or soft caress can indicate the nature of what lies ahead.

Chernobog: the dark, accursed deity, thought to summon demons to his bidding

Chervona Ruta or fern flower: on Kupalle night, it is said that the magical fern's fronds will turn from yellow to red. In the face of demons, which would lead you astray, you must remain resolute and grasp the flower, having passed a certain test. Power to see beneath the soil will then be yours, enabling you to discover treasure.

Draniki: potato cakes (grated then fried) – usually served with sour cream

Dzyady: Belarus' Day of the Dead, when families pay their respects at the graves of relatives. The spirits of the departed are thought to revisit their loved ones in the form of birds, to comfort them in grief or to warn of danger.

Kaliady: a pagan celebration of the end of year. The name may come from the Latin 'Calendae' or the word 'Kola' (wheel) - relating to the turn of the year. 'Yule' is an Anglo-Saxon word for wheel.

Karavai: the wedding loaf, large and round, decorated with dough birds and flowers. Tugged into two during the marriage ceremony by the bride and groom. Whoever possesses the larger share will 'rule' the home.

Karavanitsas: those who bake the wedding loaf.

Khorovod: a combination of a traditional circle dancing and chorus singing

Korovki: pastries shaped as cows or goats for the festive season

Kulaha: a pudding made of wheat

Kupalle Night: celebrated since pagan times, in June, coinciding with the summer solstice. It is a time of magic, of forecasting the future, and of revelling in the power of nature, water and fire. Under cover of darkness, all manner of lusty behaviour is indulged. Amidst this gaiety, it is also a time for evil creatures to roam, intent on havoc. Animals are kept safely in their barns, with talismans hanging to protect them. People who wander in meadow and forest are wise to keep their wits about them.

Perelesnik: a fiend able to take any human form, with the intention of seducing its victim, then performing an act of violence.

Pirozhki: small baked or fried pies, filled with vegetables, meat or fruit

Samogon: a strongly alcoholic drink distilled from fermented potatoes and beets, with herbs and juniper often added (similar to vodka).

Sarafan: a full skirted, long pinafore dress, often embroidered, under which a blouse is worn

Vareniki: dumplings stuffed with berries

ABOUT THE AUTHOR

Emmanuelle de Maupassant lives with her husband (maker of tea and fruit cake) and her hairy pudding terrier (connoisseur of squeaky toys and bacon treats).

Find her on Twitter and Facebook
Send her a hello. Tag her in a review.
Give her a wave, and she'll wave back.

Visit Emmanuelle's website to sign up to her newsletter
- news of sales, plus gossip and giveaways, and first eyes
on new releases, delivered to your inbox.

www.emmanuelledemaupassant.com

For behind the scenes chat, you may like to join
Emmanuelle's Boudoir, on Facebook.

BONUS MATERIAL

'DORCHADAS HOUSE'

YEARNING FOR NEW SURROUNDS, Iris Muir accepts a position at historic Dorchadas House, on the remote Scottish island of Eirig. Drawn to the wild landscape, Iris hopes to forget the burdens of her past: her father's death, a narrow life in a small-minded town.

But the dilapidated manor houses its own secrets.

There are strange cries in the night, and is the stoic housekeeper Mrs McInnes all she seems? Iris begins to have disturbing dreams about the maze, planted centuries ago in the manor grounds to honour the 'old ways', concealing something even older.

"Even on that first night, I dreamt. A
presence, in the darkness."

Despite the consuming task of refurbishing the manor as a guesthouse, Iris increasingly feels the brooding presence of Neas and Eachinn, the two brutish farmhands who seem as much a part of Dorchadas House as the old maze.

As autumn wanes and Samhain Eve approaches, the island folk prepare to honour the dead and the Goddess Nicneven, as they have done for generations past.

"The women play their part, too. We're the
most important, you could say ..."

Has something more than chance drawn her to Eirig?

Prologue

THE BOAT APPROACHED the cliffs on the eastern side of the island. Sheer rock, softening into hills. Although I'd never been to Eirig, I felt a sense of familiarity. We journeyed on, until the harbour came into sight, a welcome calm after the choppiness of the open sea.

With its row of low stone cottages along the shore, and lobster creels on the jetty, Eirig was just as I'd imagined it would be, down to the tang of seaweed cast high upon the beach, decaying in the autumn sun, and the call of cormorants overhead.

Whatever I was, or had been, I would leave behind. My old self was like the waves which had moved beyond the boat, their crests becoming indistinct, dwindling in the distance.

I would forget, and there would be no one here to cause me to remember.

∼

WHAT WAS I HOPING FOR? To escape? From the young curate, simpering love poetry as he held my hand limply in his? From the butcher's son, smelling of blood? He'd taken me to the pictures once, pushing his hand under my skirt. All I could think of was the old meat lingering under his nails.

My mother had been an only child and my father not an Inverary-man. There was no-one to dispute my claim upon our house. A desirable property, looking across the harbour. It would bring a tidy sum.

'You shouldna be so picky,' my neighbour said. 'There's few enough men to choose from and plenty enough widows. All those soldiers lost in the war; you'll have to take what ye can get, or you'll end up a spinster.'

Even in church there was no peace. Too many eyes, watching, judging, waiting for me to marry. My father was barely in his grave. He was unwell for so long I can hardly remember the man who daily saluted the calendar print of King George VI, framed upon the wall, and who took my mother dancing on a Saturday evening.

So many months of nursing him. Waking, he'd cry out for her.

'Don't worry, Da, she's resting next door,' I'd say. 'You'll see her soon.'

He'd whimper, from the pain, and I'd hold his hand.

'I'm here, Da.'

When he slept, I'd stand at the window, looking out. I made cups of tea that were cold by the time I thought to drink them. A shadow crept over me, and I'd think about the poison in the pantry cupboard. A spoonful in a dram of whisky would do it. He need drink only half.

I saw the danger. How long before the compulsion overtook me?

I told the doctor that I'd found him cold, taking up his kipper that last morning. He must have passed in the night. Whatever guilt I felt, I tempered it with knowledge of my many months of care. He'd been forced into intimacies with me that no man should endure from a woman not his wife. It had shamed him at first, and he'd clutched at the covers when I came to wash him. By the end, he barely knew what I did for him.

In the days that followed, I looked for grief to arrive, for tears, or anger. I loved him, didn't I? Instead, I was relieved. I'd been set free.

Inverary is a pretty place, with its white-washed town houses looking down the loch, but I could think only of leaving. To go where, I couldn't say. I took out the map and looked at the names. I'd never been to Glasgow. I

5

wondered how I might like to live there. The anonymity of a city appealed to me, but I doubted I could bear the noise, or the dirt, or the crowds upon the street.

It was in that mood, of indecisive determination, that I saw the advertisement in the Hebridean Chronicle.

Personal assistant sought to help in the running of Dorchadas House, on the island of Eirig: a retreat for women of an independent mind.

Eirig. It's sheep the place is known for, mostly, out on the hills. There would be space to think. In going where I was unknown, I might discover who it was I wanted to be. I took up my pen to apply, and Mrs McInnes replied within the fortnight.

Dorchadas House is quite grand. A sheltered spot, with a walled garden. Twenty bedrooms, though only a handful in use. We envisage attracting women writers and artists, and those who enjoy the outdoor life, who will take pleasure in exploring Eirig's remote, natural beauty.

Beyond that provided by the house's oil-fuelled generator, Mrs McInnes' letter explained, Eirig had no electricity. The postal office had the telegraph, but no telephone line. The packet boat came once a week with deliveries.

I was to begin on the first of the new month, with accommodation and meals provided, and a modest wage. My duties were reasonable. Only occasional cooking, and no cleaning. There were women from the village for that, and men for the heavy work. I'd oversee the decoration of the bedrooms. New wallpapers had been ordered. There were several hand-weavers on the island, making cloth for bedspreads and curtains. One thing they were not short of was wool. The old crafts might be dying on the mainland, but the peddle looms still had their place on Eirig.

The main part of my work would come later: placing invitations in the relevant periodicals, to entice suitable guests, organizing the boat to take them to and fro, from Oban. I'd manage the bookings, and see that our visitors had everything to ensure their comfort. I'd be an assistant to Mrs McInnes, in running the house.

If I found myself unsuited to island life, she assured me I'd be free to leave with a month's notice.

There was little I regretted leaving behind. My clothes fitted into two small cases and I wore the heaviest: a green sweater and good quality skirt of brown tweed, which had been my mother's. My winter coat had been hers too. With my stoutest shoes, and my beret, scarf and gloves, I was ready to face whatever the Western Isles had in store for me.

The boat met me as agreed, at Inverary Harbour, smelling strongly of fish. It was, like its captain, salt-ravaged by the waves and wind. Buchanan introduced himself, tying to the pier only long enough for me to step on board. There was no one to see me off, but he said nothing of it, nodding to the stern as he took my bag.

'Sit ye inside. The sea's a wee bit rough, but we'll manage. Ye'll not be sick I hope.'

I'd not travelled beyond the loch before, never into the open sea. No matter if I were to be sick, I was heading to

Eirig and I thrilled to the thought of it. As Inverary grew smaller behind us, the burden of so much I'd carried eased, blown by the breeze pushing us out with the tide. From the boat, the hills were more magnificent, and the birds' cries more piercing, as if my ears and eyes had come alive, and wished to take in everything anew.

Leaving behind the mouth of the loch, the boat heaved and rolled, but it was not as bad as I'd feared.

'Look at the horizon, lassie,' Captain Buchanan had advised. 'There's a blanket there for ye, and a flask. It'll be some four hours to reach Eirig, and I'll drop the creels as we go. The crab are good this season.'

He said little more on the journey, only pointing out the jagged tops of the Cuillins, on the distant Isle of Skye, as we travelled south-west. Once we were on the wildest expanse of the Minch, I did my best to hold on, and not be sent sprawling.

I was glad of the blanket and the sweet cocoa, for the damp of the sea air penetrated my coat too easily. By the time the outline of Eirig appeared, the chill was in my bones.

Nevertheless, my heart leapt to see Eirig's cliffs come into sight, violet dark, with the sun sinking to touch them. The past was a distant land and this, my new home.

CAPTAIN BUCHANAN LIFTED my bags ashore and nodded to a horse-drawn trap waiting.

'My girl, Mhairi, will take you up to the house.'

Stroking the nose of the horse was a young woman,

wrapped tight in a shawl over her dark dress. She watched as I walked unsteadily, my legs still in motion with the sea.

'It's kind of you to come,' I said, wishing to start off on a good foot. She was about my own age; there was the possibility of friendship.

'Mrs McInnes sent me,' she replied, implying that she wouldn't have bothered if the choice had been her own.

'Thank you, nonetheless.'

I returned her coolness with what I hoped was a disarming smile. 'I'm Iris, and very pleased to meet you.'

She had the grace to lend me her hand as I stepped up to sit on the trap. There were few motor vehicles in Inverary; perhaps none here.

'I like your coat,' said Mhairi, her eyes appraising my attire.

Her tone was wistful rather than envious. Her own clothing was serviceable but drab, her skirt much longer than was fashionable.

'Let's get going then,' she said, rising to join me.

We set off on a fair track, leading from the harbour, southwards, the sea to our left. Mhairi pulled an apple from her pocket and offered it to me but I shook my head. I was hungry, but there would be a supper for me at the house, I felt sure.

She shrugged and took a bite herself.

There were a great many sheep grazing, hardly lifting their heads as we passed, intent on their grassy meal. Those on the track shuffled out of the way as we approached, looking indignant rather than afraid.

'Do you have sheep yourself?' I asked, eager to engage her in conversation.

'A few. It's what we mostly do here: raise sheep. They go to market at the end of the summer. My Da and the others take them on their boats. We keep the best for tupping, o' course.'

'Tupping?'

'When we let the ram at the ewes! Don't you know anything?'

I blushed, from the embarrassment of ignorance rather than from prudery. I'd have to learn more of farming ways.

'But your father fishes?' I answered, thinking it best to turn the conversation.

'Aye, though he can only go to sea, if the weather permits. 'Tis been a good few months for the crab and lobster, and the langoustine. Those fetch the best prices in Oban. Some o' the others fish regular, with nets. There's a smokehouse up at Dorchadas, where they hang the mackerel and haddock.'

She paused to take a bite of the apple.

'There's the orchard too, o'course, behind the big house. They sell a few but we mostly eat these'ns ourselves. Mrs McInnes makes a good cider.'

I listened to the steady creak of the trap's wheels turning, and the rhythm of the horse's hooves. Grazing sheep glowed pale in the mauve twilight.

'Do you have children?'

As soon as it was out of my mouth I regretted it. I hated to be asked personal questions, or for others to make assumptions about me, as to whether I should be married, or how I should be conducting myself.

Mhairi seemed happy to answer, however.

'O aye, I've a bairn three years old. He's right bonny. I keep house for my father, and it suits us right enough. My mother and younger brother passed, so it's just us now.'

She flicked the reins to urge on the horses.

I couldn't help but notice her left hand, and the wedding band that wasn't there.

'I don't need a husband,' she said curtly, seeing my glance. 'I'm happy as I am.' She looked sideways at me, her eyes mischievous. 'I can get what I need from men without being married to one.' She shook her hair behind her, as if to emphasize her carefree state.

Where I'd nursed resentment at being judged for my spinsterhood, Mhairi was at ease in hers. An impulse to laugh rose in me and came out in a bark, which made her stare in surprise.

'You an' me might get along,' said Mhairi.

She'd bitten her apple down to the pips, which she spat into the verge.

DORCHADAS HOUSE IS NOW available from all sales outlets.

Click here to read on

ABOUT THE EDITOR

Adrea Kore is a Melbourne-based freelance writer, performer, editor and former stage director. She holds a BA (Hons) in theatre studies.

Through her fiction and non-fiction writing, she engages with the rich diversity of feminine sexuality, focusing her sometimes subversive lens on themes of desire, fantasy, and relating. She is intrigued by both the transcendent and transgressive aspects of sexuality.

After many years interpreting play-texts as a theatre director, Adrea is now applying those skills in sensing the spine of a story, and enhancing the writer's voice through developmental and structural editing. This is her first major editing project.

Adrea's erotic short stories and poetry and have appeared in various anthologies, including **Coming Together: In Verse** (2015) and **Licked** (House of Erotica 2015), **The Mammoth Book of Best New Erotica 13**, and in **A Storytelling of Ravens** (Little Raven 2014). Her provocative flash fiction and short stores have also featured online at *Bright Desire*, *For the Girls*, *Little Raven* and for the infamous fiction gallery of the *Erotica Readers and Writers Association.* In another guise, her work has also appeared in *Etchings* literary journal (2013). Currently she is working on her first collection of themed erotic short stories *Watching You Watching Me* and a novella.

To discover more, visit her at:

https://koredesires.wordpress.com/about/
https://www.facebook.com/adrea.kore
https://twitter.com/adrea_kore

Printed in Great
Britain
by Amazon